THE RAT REVEREND
CLANCY & THE 7
SACRAMENTS

DAVID L. CARTER

APOCRYPHILE
PRESS

This one is for Mary Spotswood Pou
June 23,1944- May 27,2002
3-D!!!!

Apocryphile Press
1100 County Route 54
Hannacroix, NY 12087
www.apocryphilepress.com

Copyright © 2021 by David L. Carter
Printed in the United States of America
ISBN 978-1-949643-81-7 | paper
ISBN 978-1-949643-82-4 | ePub

Please join our mailing list at
www.apocryphilepress.com/free
We'll keep you up-to-date on all our new releases,
and we'll also send you a FREE BOOK.
Visit us today!

CONTENTS

1. Holy Orders   1
2. Extreme Unction   26
3. Baptism   53
4. Holy Matrimony   80
5. Confirmation   129
6. Penance   146
7. Holy Communion   181
   Coda   194

HOLY ORDERS

A bruptly, the dream ended. Clancy opened his eyes and found himself standing up on his hind legs, his forelegs upraised and outspread, just like Reverend DeBassompierre in the act of benediction. "Yes Lord!" Clancy cried in his high-pitched squeak—for he was a young rat—"Thy will be done!"

Clancy lived in the cellar of St. Aloysius Episcopal Church. Of course he was obliged to keep himself out of sight of the human beings who comprised the staff and the congregation of the church, but as a Christian, Clancy did often make his way upstairs out of the cellar into the church proper to observe the various ministries, especially Sunday Services. But it had certainly never seriously crossed Clancy's mind that he could ever preach the Gospel like the young and handsome rector of St. Aloysius, Reverend Silas DeBassompierre, MDiv, ThD.

But what else was he to make of this dream, from which he'd just awakened, fully upright?

He'd dreamt that he was in an enormous room, very dark and full of hidden dangers, and that the only way that he could stay safe was to hide in the corner. But a voice rang out, and it was that of Reverend DeBassompierre himself, calling Clancy by name. Now, Clancy was well aware—his dear departed Great-Aunt November had many times reminded him—that humans did not know how to share, and so did not and must never know that there were rats in the cellar of their churches. Hence, in waking life Rev. DeBassompierre had no idea that Clancy existed, and certainly did not know his name. And yet, in Clancy's dream, the Reverend was summoning him! "Clancy!" the Reverend had called, in that low and heavy voice which had a lulling quality that was pleasing to Clancy but soporific for the congregation. "Come in out of the darkness!"

In his dreams, as well as in the waking world, the Reverend was, to Clancy, magnificent. So wise and solemn, with a presence remarkably austere for such a young priest, and yet he had a rare but winning smile. And in Clancy's dream, that smile shone out in the darkness, and the darkness comprehended it not. "Yes!" the fascinated rodent cried out. "I'm here! What can I do?"

"Spread the word," said the Reverend. "Feed my sheep." And with that the darkness of the corner in which Clancy hid was dispelled, and Clancy was soon scooped up into the palm of a warm and gentle human hand that lifted him high into an ever intensifying light. And the hand, he knew, somehow belonged at once to the Reverend and to the Lord. He woke up then, in that ancient and modern attitude of blessing, and he knew that this was no ordinary dream, that he had in fact been called —by God.

৩৯৩

"PRAISE THE LORD!" he breathed. This was a favorite phrase of his dear Aunt November, who had been raised in the cellar of a Southern Baptist church. How he wished she was still here, to share his joy in having been chosen for ministry.

Since his Aunt November's passing, Clancy had one other soul to talk to, and that was Hertz, an earthworm who lived in the composter that produced fresh mulch for the community garden of St. Aloysius. It was with Hertz, then, that Clancy shared his vision.

"Hertz!" he cried, after wriggling out of the cellar through the gap under the door and scampering around the corner of the church's administrative wing to the tapered composter at the edge of the garden. It was still early in the morning, with dew upon the grass, and neither Reverend DeBassompierre nor Grace, his administrative assistant, had yet arrived. "Hertz! Are you here? Are you busy? Oh, Hertz, I have the most amazing news! I've been called to preach!"

There was no immediate response from within the composter. Clancy crouched in the shadow of that strong smelling plastic structure, shaped rather like a blunt inverted pyramid on short plastic legs, and waited. In the mornings Hertz was often grouchy and reluctant to converse. That was just his way. Clancy waited a few moments, looking around at the large backyard of the church, at the community garden, the flat sandy graveyard, and the playground. Beyond that was the forest, which went on forever, as far as Clancy knew. He could hear the swift whoosh of traffic rushing along the boulevard in front of the church, and accompanying that background noise he heard the variegated songs of birds, as well as a distant train whistle. It was a bright, crisp spring morning, and he didn't believe he'd ever felt so good.

How he wanted to share his good news with his best friend! He stuck his snout into one of the ventilator slots in the casing of the compost bin and squealed happily at his friend through the rotting food and damp mulch. "Hertz! Oh, Hertz, I hate to bug you, but I've been CALLED!"

Clancy could see, among the sludge and soil and the rotting vegetables and table scraps and coffee grounds, a whole colony of earthworms hard at work revivifying soil, but he did not see his friend, their patriarch, among them. Where in earth was he? "Hertz!" He cried again.

From the very depths of the composter, where he preferred

to spend most of his day in a largish chamber that he'd prepared for himself as a center of operations, Hertz the Elder Earthworm heard the squeaking voice of the furry creature that had many moons before saved him from an untimely demise when he'd first come to St. Aloysius, stuck on the shoe of a tipsy (and thus oblivious) Reverend DeBassompierre. Knowing the rodent wouldn't rest until he'd had his say, the earthworm made his way to the topsoil of the composter and stuck his tip out. "I'm right here!" the earthworm grumbled. "For Ground's sake! What is it? We're in the middle of a huge input, here. We've got to get this garbage broken down before it starts to stink to high heaven and draws those stupid raccoons..."

"I'm sorry, Hertz," Clancy said happily. He was more than accustomed to his dearest friend's prickliness. "I just had to talk to somebody! Hertz, I've been called! I've been called to preach, Hertz! I'm going to spread the Gospel!" Clancy wrung his front paws with excitement, and his black eyes glistened with zeal.

"Great," said the earthworm drily. "Congratulations. I'm sure you'll be a great success. At least better than that boring old DeBassoon. Now, let me get back to..."

"Wait, Hertz...wait! Just for a little bit, if you can! I won't keep you for long, but I need your help! I was wondering, Hertz, do you think I could possibly hold a service here? At least one time? See, I don't have a church, or anywhere to preach. So I thought maybe I could preach right here? I mean, it's the perfect spot if you think about it... right here in the shade... and it's easy for anybody who might be around to see from the yard, and easy to get to...but not so out in the open that I would be nervous. You know I'm not used to being outside. And not that I want you to feel any pressure, I know you're always real busy, but if you did want to listen to me preach, you wouldn't have to go anywhere, because the church would be right here! But I'll find somewhere else if you want me to, Hertz. After all, this is your home..."

Hertz knew that if he didn't nip this foolishness in the bud right away, he would only have himself to blame. He peered down with his rudimentary vision at the furry creature in the shadow of the composter and summoned all of his disdain.

But he couldn't do it. The rat, after all, had saved his life once upon a time, when, flung from the toe of the Reverend's shoe, he'd found himself on the dry inanimate aisle carpet in the sanctuary of St. Aloysius Church. He would have dried up and died had Clancy not discovered him and nursed him back to health in the soil of a potted fern. He decided it would be best to allow but not encourage.

"It's a free country. When do you plan on starting this church?"

"Why, this Sunday! This coming Sunday!" He clasped his paws together with pious glee. "Oh, I'm so excited." His joy irrepressible, he lifted himself onto his hind legs and kissed his dear friend on the tip. "Oh Hertz! Bless you! Just think! You can consider yourself the very first member, the founding member—unless you count me—of St. Aloysius Jr. Church! God is so good!"

And with that, Clancy scampered back to the cellar of the church to plan his very first sermon, leaving the worm to withdraw back into his beloved stench and solitude, feeling—not for the first time in their long friendship—that he'd been too soft on the rat.

☙✦❧

THAT EVENING, after Reverend DeBassompierre and Grace went home, Clancy stole out from behind the Reverend's bookshelf, where he'd spent, as usual, much of his afternoon observing the Reverend at his studies. He scurried down the hallway to the chapel for his usual sweet hour of prayer. Positioning himself reverently before the empty altar, he addressed the crucifix that hung on thin but strong wire from the rafter above. This was his beloved Savior, always there for him.

"Dear Lord..." he began. "Thank you so, so much for calling me! I'm so excited I don't know what to do! But I promise I'm going to do everything I can to glorify Your Name and spread Your Word. And Lord, thank you for good old Hertz. I know he doesn't like it when things change, so it's real nice of him to let me have my first service right there where he lives. And Lord! What a role model in Reverend DeBassompierre! This afternoon he even practiced his sermon! I know I'll never be as smart or as deep in the Word as he is, but at least I know what passage to preach on this Sunday! Everything is just coming together like a miracle, Lord, and I guess that's just exactly what it is! All I ask, Lord is that you send me a Spirit of Calmness once we get closer to Sunday. Because I know I'm already getting nervous, Lord...What if I can't think of anything to say? I guess, Lord, that all I can do is leave it in Your hands. After all, you are the One that called me!

৩৩৩

WHEN SUNDAY DAWNED, it was, to Clancy's consternation, inauspicious weather, not without a good deal of wind and rain, and just before dawn there was even a brief spell of thunder and lightning. And yet Clancy was heartened when the cars of the original St. Aloysius' congregation began to fill up the parking lot, as they did every Sunday morning at just before ten o'clock, rain or shine. From his sleeping spot on a bundle of old and slightly moldy choir robes dumped in the corner of the cellar years before, Clancy could hear the humans filing into the sanctuary, just as he had on every previous Sunday of his life. He rose and stretched and yawned and made his way to and through the cheap plywood crawlspace door that opened out onto the churchyard. Aunt November had chewed a small space out of the bottom corner that Clancy still wasn't too stout yet to squeeze through. He peered out. A big raindrop from the power-line above hit his snout, and this alarmed him and made him squeal. He had to take a moment to compose and center himself. He couldn't help but be puzzled that the Lord did not arrange for nicer weather on the occasion of his very first service, but he told himself that God had not said this would be easy.

By the time he reached the composter his fur was damp with drizzle, and he was not a little chilly, but it could have been worse, and he was undaunted. He scrambled up the frame of the composter and perched on the top edge, overlooking the garden, the graveyard, the rarely used playground, and the dense woods beyond. The composter was as good a platform as he could have wished for...even if it was quite smelly—and at the top of his high and penetrating voice, he delivered the following announcement, to whomever might be around to hear.

"Good Morning!" He looked down and he was gratified, though not surprised, to see the tips of several worms, among them Hertz's, poking out of the ventilation holes in the casing of the middle drawer of the composter. "Good morning, and God bless you. I'm here to announce that in just a few minutes, the very first official service of St. Aloysius Jr. Episcopal Church will begin. I'm Reverend Clancy, and I am going to be your preacher and pastor for as long as you will have me. I want to take this moment to invite anyone around the churchyard who can hear me to join us as we come together, here at this holy altar, to learn about and to worship, in scripture, sermon, and song, our Lord and Savior Jesus Christ. Now, I know that most of us who aren't human aren't Christians either, and that some of us don't even know what a Christian is, but that doesn't mean that Jesus doesn't love us and doesn't save us if we ask Him to. And Jesus wants us to know Him and love Him as much as He loves us, and that's why I'm here with you, to share the good news with any creature who wants to come hear it. All are welcome. No matter what. So, if you can hear me, come closer, no one is going to hurt you, and be sure to introduce yourself after the service, and of course tell all your friends and family that they are welcome too. Now. Let's get started..."

Clancy held out his front paws to the dreary surroundings in that classic gesture of benediction. "The LORD be with you!"

He paused. He heard no response other than the distant mush of wet tires on the boulevard.

"And also with me," he said.

From there, Reverend Clancy did his best to follow the rubric as he'd beheld it so many times before. He sang the only hymn he knew well enough to sing in its entirety—*Onward Christian Soldiers*, which had been his Aunt November's very favorite. Then he recited the Scripture readings he'd heard Reverend DeBassompierre go over earlier in the week—the Old Testament passage describing the binding of Isaac, the 53rd Psalm, 1st Corinthians Chapter 13, and finally, from the Gospel, the Sermon on the Mount. Then it was time for his own sermon. He took a deep breath and looked around again. Apart from the worms just beneath him there was no indication that anyone else was listening. The sky above was low and grey. The trees in the distance were like an uncomprehending, distant and standoffish crowd of onlookers. And yet to Clancy it seemed as if there was something hushed and hidden but still present and interested nearby. He lifted one paw, made the sign of the cross against his front, and, invoking the names of the Father, the Son, and the Holy Ghost, he began to preach.

"Dear friends..." he said. "Welcome again to St. Aloysius Jr. I'm Reverend Clancy, like I said, and I'm so happy to be your pastor, and I want you all to know that I am here for you as a friend and a helper, whenever you need me. I live in the cellar of the big church, and right around the corner there you can see the little door. There's a corner missing, and if you are small enough you can squeeze through it. So come see me any time, or if you can't fit through, just call me and I'll come out. I don't mind. After all, what it means to be a Christian is that we will bear each other's burdens, and treat each other the way we want to be treated. Because, like Jesus said in the Gospel story that I just read you, 'the meek shall inherit the earth.'

"Now, friends, what that means, is that it is just so important to the Lord that we try to be nice. And Lord knows, that isn't always easy. Why, if you know the Bible, then you know that even the Lord lost His temper sometimes, especially with the Pharisees, who were people who were out to get him, but sometimes he even got upset with his friends and family! The Lord understands that sometimes we aren't at our best. But He wants us to be nice and meek whenever we possibly can. Because, if we feel too important, then we don't appreciate what's around us! And that's a terrible thing. We should always be grateful for our blessings. After all, you can ask yourself, how would you feel if you gave someone something that you thought they would like, and they threw it away because they would rather have something else? Well, you'd feel terrible, wouldn't you? You would feel like you weren't appreciated, and that you couldn't do anything to please that person. Now, is that how we want the Lord to feel about us? Like we can't be satisfied? Well, of course not! No one wants to be too hard to please! And the Lord wants us to be pleased, and to love Him AND the world He made for us to live in! We just have to trust that He knows what we need and when we need it. And when He decides it's the right time, He will provide! After all He is in charge, and He knows so much more than we ever can about what's best for us. We need to remember that we have a Father in Heaven that loves us just as much as He loves human beings. And that's why it's so important that the rest of us have a place to come to—to remind ourselves that we aren't just dumb creatures. And that's why the Lord has called me to start this church! To bring us all together, so that we can help one another through good times and bad. That's what it means, friends, to be meek. It means that we know that we need help sometimes, and that we need each other and we need the Lord. When we have each other, we'll inherit the earth! That's why I'm so happy, because I can stand up here and say to you that I'm your pastor and your friend and that I welcome you, and anyone else who wants to come, to Sunday services at St.

Aloysius Jr. Church, a community of the meek. And now, if you'll join me as our Savior taught us to pray, Our Father, Who art in Heaven..."

Such was the essence of Clancy's very first Sunday sermon, preached in spite of and alongside the dismal weather. After the Lord's Prayer he looked over the seemingly empty landscape. By all appearances not a soul, apart from himself and a few worms, had heard one word of his homily. And yet Clancy, with eternal optimism and a sixth sense, still felt quite strongly that he had been and was being regarded closely by a presence that he could not see. He stood up on his hind legs for as long as he could and gazed from east to west. Rain, clouds, parked cars, and in the distance, the trees that were the woods were all that he could make out. Not even the usual sparrows and pigeons and squirrels who could sometimes be seen going about their business in the churchyard and surroundings were out and about on this inclement morning. Clancy took in a breath with which to deliver the dismissal, when he happened to look towards the playground and noticed a crouching form. Underneath the low slope of the plastic swing set slide, he saw the glinting eyes and baleful, broad and unblinking countenance of a cat.

Clancy's blood froze in his veins. His immediate instinct was to run, to flee, to burrow, to hide. This was the stuff of nightmares. It was true, and fortunate, that the Beast did not advance. But nevertheless, its crouch, its gaze, its very presence, everything about it seemed poised to attack and devour without mercy. Utterly forgetting to pronounce the final blessing, Clancy leaped off of the composter and scrambled as fast as he could back to the safety of his cellar.

THE REMAINDER of that Sunday was a time of trial for Clancy. On the one paw, a clear call to ministry. On the other paw...a cat! What in the world was he going to do? Clancy had a nervous habit, ever since early childhood, of attempting to soothe himself in stressful times by gnawing on the end of his long, hairless tough-skinned tail, and by the time he went to sleep that night, his poor tail end was raw and bloody and throbbing. The next day, even though it was Reverend DeBassompierre's day off as well as Grace's and he had the whole building to himself, he didn't stir from the cellar until well after noon. He crept up the stairs and underneath the door that opened into the main corridor that connected the sanctuary to the administration suite, and paused just to make extra sure he was alone. Never in his memory had he ever felt so insecure within St. Aloysius. His intention was to make his way to the Chapel to pray before the altar, but as if with a mind of their own, his paws led him to the Reverend's office.

He climbed into the cushioned armless chair across the desk from the Reverend's plush leather office swivel chair, and found himself addressing, not the Lord, but the absent Reverend. "Oh, Reverend DeBassompierre! What should I do? What would you do, if you were me?"

Of course there was no answer. As never before in his life, Clancy felt utterly on his own, uncertain of his deepest convictions. Was he supposed to start this church, or wasn't he?! The poor attendance at the service was one thing...after all, it was only the first one, and on a rainy day at that...but the presence of that cat was another. Of course he should have known—his Aunt November had always told him—that the world outside the walls of a good solid church was a world full of dangers, temptations, and ruthless predators. But—he protested to the image and essence of his beloved Aunt in his mind—the Lord *called* me!

Aunt November, he imagined, would have likely responded to that with a prim silence that could dampen lightning. She had always praised her nephew's intelligence, piety and deportment, but as one would praise the qualities of an infant or a pet, as potentials and not actualities. The Lord would not have called him to preach outdoors while Aunt November was among the living, of that Clancy was sure, and for that he was grateful. It would have upset the dear lady for him to spend that much time exposed.

It took a moment, but it took. Well, of course! Clancy realized. There's nothing to be afraid of! The Lord knows what He's doing! To everything there is a season, as the Bible says, and as the Lord says, get thee behind me Satan, for my time has not yet come. The Lord knew better than to call me to ministry when it would worry Aunt November and stir up strife between us, and He knows what cats are like. He hasn't brought me this far, though, just to feed me to that Beast! God will find a way!

Renewed zeal propelled him off of the chair, and he made several laps around the office, so suddenly re-energized was he. He loved these bursts of energy, for he was well aware that he was a sedentary rat by nature, and prone to stoutness. As he scampered he leaped for joy. He would trust in the Lord no matter what.

Still, he figured it wouldn't hurt to discuss the whole thing with Hertz. Hertz was almost as smart as Reverend DeBassompierre, and when it came to keeping safe, maybe more so. He would talk to Hertz. Right now.

Before he left the office, though, he hopped back onto the Reverend's desk to peer out the window at the swing set. He saw with relief that no cat was there.

❧

"Well, you better give it up, then," the worm warned, "if you don't want to end up as Sunday dinner."

"Oh, Hertz." Clancy found he wasn't surprised that Hertz was inclined to be defeatist. "You know I can't do that. The *Lord* called me."

Hertz knew he should never have allowed the rat to talk him into all of this ridiculous and now apparently dangerous church business. If a cat was anywhere near, that did not bode well for any rat, God notwithstanding. But when Clancy felt he was being led by the 'Lord,' there was no getting through to him. Unless you went through the 'Lord' business to get there. "Listen," said the worm. "Don't you think the Lord might be telling you to forget it? Think about it! No one showed up but a predator—that ought to tell you something! You know, you've had it soft for so long that you don't really know what it's like out here. Why do you think the humans wrap themselves up like they do and build their buildings? They know they don't stand a chance out in the open, and neither do you. Look at me. I know my place. There's not a robin alive that isn't looking to gobble up a nice big fat worm like me. And they're always poking around. But as long as I keep my tail inside this composter, they can't get me. If you don't want to get gobbled up, you have to have protection. What have you got?"

Clancy's every strand of fur, including his whiskers, stiffened. Although he had not misunderstood his friend's warning, he knew it was really the Lord, working in His usual mysterious way through the worm's habitual naysaying, not to discourage, but to challenge.

"Hertz!" He squealed. "That's it! You're right! The Lord is giving me a sign! I was so scared and nervous I couldn't see! I just need to put on the armor of GOD! No one...not even a cat...I *think*...can reject the Love of God. AND GOD WANTS THAT CAT TO BE REDEEMED! Oh, thank you, Hertz! Thank you!"

Hertz knew when he was beaten. He withdrew, and it was not a little while before the Clancy even noticed that his friend was no longer present.

෴

THAT EVENING, in the dark, familiar sanctuary, Clancy said his prayers. "Lord," he prayed, "I haven't been very trusting, have I? I know it's all in Your hands. I let my fears get the better of me last Sunday, and I'm so sorry. But I praise You for putting Hertz in my life, because he has so much good sense, just like Aunt November used to have. I am so blessed. All I ask of You now, Lord, is that You will watch over me when I meet that cat, that You will guide my way and guard my tongue. I don't want to say the wrong thing, Lord, the way I do sometimes when I'm nervous. I just want to show Your grace any way I can. So be with me, Lord. Because I think that maybe this is my David and Goliath moment. But the only stone I want to throw is Your Love."

⚜

BUT THE FOLLOWING SUNDAY SERVICE, in which he preached upon the text from Matthew in which Christ exhorts His followers to love their enemies and pray for those who persecute them, passed without any sign of a cat, before, during, or after. As a matter of fact, after a couple more Sundays Clancy practically forgot all about the cat, because, to his surprise and delight, his ministry was slowly and surely extending its reach. Exactly how the Word was spread he was never to be sure, but the fact was that a number of creatures who made their homes or haunts in the area surrounding St. Aloysius couldn't help but notice and become intrigued by the weekly spectacle of an audacious rat proclaiming its curious and fantastic doctrine to all who might hear, and some bolder specimens began to draw nearer. Clancy's first converts were a pair of pigeons, whom he'd seen from time to time before his calling, perched on the service wire that ran from the utility pole at the end of the church's gravel parking lot to the corner of the roof of the administrative wing. Noting that they seemed to be listening to his sermon, he called up to them afterwards, introduced himself, and after some conversation, mainly with the female, Clancy thought that their rich warbling voices were so lovely that he immediately asked them if they would be interested in serving as the choir. The female, whose name was Ottoline, demurred. But when Clancy persisted and pleaded in his winsome way, she found herself accepting, with not a little pleasure. Clancy arranged to meet with the couple on Wednesday evenings for choir practice. There were several, actually up to a dozen squirrels who never actually introduced themselves, but who began to attend with regularity, and while the younger ones among these were restless congregants who disrupted his sermons every now and then by suddenly dashing away as if they simply could not remain still for another moment, Clancy was glad to have them show up. Hertz, of course, could not avoid attending, and while he maintained that Clancy's invisible God was the last thing on his mind, he had to admit that the rodent was on a roll. He was wary of that pigeon couple, Ottoline and Steve, but Clancy assured him that Ottoline and Steve were by nature and taste vegetarians. "They only eat seeds," he said. "I asked them. You don't think I'd let anything happen to you and your family, do you, Hertz?"

"What makes you think you could stop 'em?" grumbled Hertz. "And maybe THEY don't eat worms, but with my luck you'll get a bunch of robins over here that do. *Then* what?!"

"I'll make sure all the newcomers know the ground rules," said Clancy. "No eating your fellow members. No exceptions. I promise you, Hertz, I won't let anyone hurt you. Don't you know that?"

Hertz did know that the rodent would never let anything happen to the colony if he could help it. But the worm knew good and well from experience that Clancy was generous to a fault.

❦

THE FOLLOWING Sunday dawned bright and clear. Glorious, in a word, and Clancy was delighted. He raised himself up on his hind legs, as soon as he was out of doors, and took in a breath of the crisp, clear spring air. Praise the Lord, he said to himself. Today's service is going to be wonderful! I can just feel it in my bones! He scampered around the corner to the composter, as carefree as if he owned the world, stopping briefly as he passed the dumpster at the end of the parking lot, for he had a feeling that something was watching him from somewhere near or even within that massive and smelly metal structure. But the feeling, which was at once pleasant and unpleasant, came and went in an instant.

When he climbed up to the top tier of the composter, he was amazed! One could not call it a packed service by any account, but to Clancy the gathering was unexpectedly and gratifyingly dense. The pigeon couple, Ottoline and Steven, were there, and there were more young squirrels than he could count scampering around. Over in the graveyard a number of crows perched on top of a collection of tombstones and seemed to be watching with interest. Clancy hoped that they were far enough away so that Hertz would not be alarmed.

"Peace be with you!" Clancy cried, and lifted up his paws in benediction. With so many newcomers in the crowd he couldn't expect everyone to know the proper response, so once again he responded to himself: "And also with me." He paused and looked around, and never had he felt so satisfied with life as he knew it. "Thank you all so much for joining me today in the worship of the Lord. What a beautiful day He hath made! Truly the Spirit is with us on this pretty Sunday morning. Let's all listen, as our St. Aloysius Jr. choir leads us in one of the newest hymns that we've learned. It's called, *God Hears*."

Clancy nodded, and he, Ottoline, and Steven began to squeal and warble and coo the hymn that Clancy had composed himself and had spent the last Wednesday evening attempting to teach them. It was hardly a polished performance, but it had spirit.

"Thank you, St. Aloysius Singers," he said as the final notes faded. "That was so beautiful. Now, a reading from the book of Daniel."

And it was at that moment, as he recounted the ancient tale of the defenseless hero cast into the den of savage beasts, that he saw in the distance, at the edge of the woods, as still as a sphinx (apart from the occasional twitch of its tail), that damn cat. Oh Lord, he thought, but he managed to get through the story of Daniel's vindication in the Lion's Den without a hitch. If anyone in the congregation noticed he was troubled, they didn't let on.

Providentially, the sermon he'd prepared for the day was short and to the point. It was based upon the Gospel reading from Matthew, in which Jesus, at the urging of his disciples, fed over five thousand people out of five loaves and two fishes. Clancy declared that there was nothing that God could not do for those who believed in his Goodness, and that there is always enough to go around as long as we are willing to share. All the while that he was preaching, of course, he was aware of the threat in the distance, that terribly still cat.

"And now," he said, once he reached his conclusion, which neatly dovetailed the feeding of the five thousand with the fasting of the lions in Daniel's story, "Let us all sing along as Ottoline and Steve lead us in my Aunt November's very favorite hymn, *Onward Christian Soldiers.*" And so saying, he hopped right off the composter into the relative shelter of its shadow, where he felt less exposed, yet still very vulnerable. He was ready for the whole service to be over so that he could get back inside the cellar. But of course he couldn't just preach and run! That would be suspicious, on top of being bad form. He expected himself, and he felt he was expected, to remain available following the service for fellowship. Especially on a day like today, with so many newcomers to welcome!

Oh Lord, he thought. *Why me?*

In the shadow of the composter, he made the sign of the cross against his white chest, then made his way into the midst of the congregation and introduced himself to one of the smaller squirrels, who was scampering back and forth in a seemingly aimless way. "Thank you for coming this morning," said Reverend Clancy. "I hope you'll join us again next Sunday!"

"Maybe I will..." said the squirrel, "but not if HE's around!!"

And with a flick of his ear, he indicated the distant and ominous feline figure.

Clancy swallowed hard. "Oh..." he said. "I'm sure he's just passing by. I don't think he'll bother us."

The squirrel chittered mirthlessly. "Maybe you're sure, but I'm not," said the squirrel. "He's got that lean and hungry look. I wish he'd go away."

Clancy did not want to either deny or affirm the squirrel's concern, lest he alienate a parishioner. He wasn't sure how to respond. But the message implicit in the squirrel's lack of openness—which mirrored his own—was all too clear. The cat might be a threat, but the challenge to himself as the pastor was to approach this threat with the love of Christ. This was, he realized with a sinking heart, a test. *Oh Lord*, he thought. *Already?*

"Don't worry," he heard himself say to the squirrel. "I'll go talk to him."

The squirrel reared itself up on its hind legs as if Clancy had breathed fire. "Are you nuts?" cried the squirrel without irony, too astonished to intend any pun. "He'll have you for lunch!"

Clancy knew the squirrel was probably right. But with the claim of God upon him, Clancy could not back down.

The squirrel looked around nervously and lowered his chittering voice. "Listen, I have to admit, I don't understand all the Jesus and God and other stuff you've been talking about, and to be honest, most of the rest of us around here don't either. It's a nice idea, I guess, that the same God or whatever you call it that lets the humans do whatever they want likes us too. And I like what you always say about looking out for each other, but when it comes to some of those big flesh eaters, you just can't be too careful. They just don't care about the little guy! Trust me! We see what goes on out here, we see it *all* from up in the trees! Besides, think about the rest of us! If you let that cat think there's easy prey around here, we'll all be dead meat. Please, Reverend, don't mess with that cat."

Clancy knew the squirrel was right. And yet, so was God. The rat had never felt so torn.

The squirrel, who well understood and recognized how, in the face of imminent danger, one can lose all sense of what direction to go in, sensed Clancy's fresh uncertainty. "Please, Reverend," he said. "Be smart." And with that, he dashed away.

"Oh Lord," Clancy said aloud. "What do you want me to do?!"

"Go inside," said a familiar, gravelly voice, which, despite its familiarity, was so unexpected that Clancy honestly thought for a moment that the Almighty was addressing him. Every single strand of fur on his pelt stood on end. Then he saw, in the ground before him, a sight as rare as it was moving. There lay Hertz, his tip slightly elevated, confronting him as he had never confronted him before. Not since the very earliest days of their acquaintance had Clancy ever known Hertz to emerge fully from the safety and moistness of the composter.

"Go home," the worm repeated. "Go back to the cellar. I mean it. Get your tail back in the church before that's all that's left of you. You know I don't hold with that Jesus of yours, but I bet if he does exist somewhere he doesn't want you to end up as cat food just when you're getting started. I'm telling you, I know what you're about to try; I know what's going on in that hairy head of yours, and you better just forget it. That cat will rip you to shreds before you get one word out of your mouth, and I don't want to have to watch it. Besides, you don't even know if he'll be able to understand you." Hertz drew himself up to Clancy's eye level and did not waver. Clancy was, within the maelstrom of his fear and trembling and determination, not a little touched. For all of Hertz's gruffness, he did care. It was almost enough to...

"Oh, Hertz," he said. "I... wish I could forget it. I really do." He wanted to gather the worm in his arms and never let him go, but he knew that Hertz would be uncomfortable with such a display. But he also knew that the chances were very great that he might never see his dearest friend again. And propelled by an impulse as solemn as it was affectionate, he leaned forward and kissed the worm gently on his tip. Hertz reared back, annoyed.

"I'm sorry, Hertz," Clancy said. "But I have to do what I believe the Lord wants me to do. I have to share the Gospel, no matter what."

The worm grew rigid with the frustration that comes from concern. "Oh Lord, Lord, Lord. That's all you care about! You don't give a damn about how your friends might feel!"

"Hertz!" Clancy was moved, but just as he was about to succumb to another ill-conceived affectionate impulse, he detected, in the periphery of his vision, a small movement at the wood's edge—so slight it could have been a mere flick of the cat's whiskers, but enough to make his blood run cold. The worm, whose eyesight was far more rudimentary than the rodent's, did not see anything, but he could sense Clancy's intensified distress. "What now?!" he said.

"You better go inside, Hertz," said Clancy. He turned now to face the woods—and his distant adversary—and forgot all about the worm, who was still beside him, though now speechless with horror. "Lord," said Clancy, "strengthen me."

And that was that. His mind made up, Clancy, to his own surprise, suddenly felt a sense...not of safety, exactly, or even of deliverance, but of trust, as if he were following a leader that he knew and trusted into battle. He had no idea what would happen; he was totally convinced, however, that his chances of survival were slim. At the same time he knew that he was doing the only thing he could live with doing if by some miracle he did survive. He felt sure now that it was not so much the will of God that he be destroyed, but rather that he must provide ministry even in the face of destruction. What happened next would be squarely in the paws of the cat...Clancy could only do his Lord's will. Genuflecting, perhaps for the last time, he then put all paws to the ground and scampered steadily forward under the open sky.

"Lord, strengthen me, Lord strengthen me, Lord strengthen me..." These words, as if with a will of their own, marched through his mind like Christian soldiers as he made his way across the churchyard. So absorbing was this image that when the cat suddenly sprang and was intercepted and knocked sideways by a figure almost half its size, Clancy wasn't immediately aware of it. It was not until the cat took off like a flash back into the dense woods that it dawned on Clancy that he'd quite literally been saved. He stopped in his tracks, looking all around, but seeing nothing in the periphery. But then he looked straight ahead and saw his rescuer—a rat, a very large and scrappy looking rat who likewise regarded him.

Clancy could only gape at this all too familiar, yet unknown figure. Having been raised by his beloved and pious Aunt November totally within the confines of the church basement, Clancy had no memory of any contact with a male of his own species. Aunt November had wanted him to grow free from any influence by any member of the family they'd left behind in the squalor of the waterfront, where Clancy's parents and their peers had lapsed into what the dear lady considered to be degeneracy. Confronted by the creature that had vanquished the cat, Clancy wondered for a moment if it really was a rat like himself. He never dreamed that a rat could be so big! Almost half as big as that cat! A large specimen it was, and not a little ferocious in aspect. It shared the cat's lean and hungry look, its beady black eyes shining with a savage intensity. As it regarded Clancy, its hairless and whiplike tail twitched as if it had a life of its own. It lifted itself up on its hind legs as if to confront Clancy with its underbelly, to display its gender, and Clancy, prompted by some deep and ineluctable instinct, did likewise. Then the two of them settled back into their natural four-legged stance and continued to regard one another.

Clancy observed the glittering dark eyes, the tufted translucent ears, the moist and snuffling nose, and the orange incisors. This was no angel of the Lord. This was precisely the type of rat

that Aunt November had always warned him of, a guttersnipe, a
ne'er-do-well. He had the fierce and confrontational air of a
survivor, a ruthless and indefatigable rebel. And yet he had saved
Clancy from a certain death—and put himself in harm's way!
"Who are you?" Clancy managed to ask. The other rat only
looked at him. Then, "Who are you?" the stranger responded,
with what seemed to Clancy to be disdain. Then he turned tail
decisively and took off in the direction of the dumpster behind
the convenience store down the street from St. Aloysius. Clancy
watched as his savior clambered up the side of that structure and
disappeared into the darkness within, slipping easily through an
opening in the sliding metal door in the side.

"Holy Mother of God," breathed Clancy, unconsciously
repeating an oath he'd heard many times from the lips of
Reverend DeBassompierre. "What in the world?!" he followed
up with an expression of Aunt November's.

It took him a moment to collect himself sufficiently to
realize that he was still in the middle of the churchyard, exposed
to any number of dangers from beyond or above. He scampered
back to the crawlspace door, but not before stopping to speak to
Hertz. "Did you see that?!" he squealed. "Did you see what just
happened?"

The worm was irritated beyond endurance with anticipated
sorrow and relief. "I wasn't paying attention," he said tersely and
testily, for indeed he had not been able to bear watching what he
was sure would be his friend's final moments. "What happened?"

"Well, Hertz! You didn't see?! It was a miracle! An honest to
goodness miracle! Oh! I was halfway across the courtyard and
that ...that... CAT! He just lunged at me...he came this close!
And I mean, Hertz, I thought I was done for! But then..."
Clancy found himself tongue-tied. He saw again, in his mind's
eye, the collision, practically right on top of him, of cat and rat,
in which the cat, caught off-guard, had been overcome by a
smaller and more solid and determined assailant. "Hertz!" he
managed to say. "It was just like David and Goliath!"

"Who?"

Clancy, not for the first or last time, looked at his worldly-wise but spiritually illiterate friend, and loved him. "Oh, Hertz. Some people from the Bible. A great King of Israel and...well, I'm not sure what exactly Goliath was. But he was big. Anyway, I just wish you had seen it. Because I was so scared that I wasn't really paying attention myself, and ...well, anyway, just when that cat was going to get me, just out of nowhere, a rat I've never seen before ran up and knocked him out of the way, and saved me! He saved me, Hertz! And ...but before I even knew what was happening, he was gone! Oh, Hertz, it was just...unbelievable. I'm telling you, it was a miracle, Hertz! It was like a...a guardian angel!" And, having come willy-nilly to this satisfying explanation, Clancy began to tremble with an overwhelming sense of blessedness.

"A guardian angel, huh," the worm said drily. "What did it look like? I suppose rat angels have bat wings?" And Hertz took some low, wormish delight in his own wit.

Clancy blinked, and became thoughtful for a moment. "No, I don't think he had any wings. All I saw was his belly, really, and his..." Here Clancy paused, feeling uncomfortably warm. Then the uncomfortable warmth passed. "But I know he was mostly brown, with a white patch on his chest, and I think his eyes were black...just an ordinary looking rat, but really big! He was just..." And here again, Clancy found himself at a loss for words.

"Sounds like you," said the worm, rather flatly.

"Me!" squeaked Clancy. "Lord, no! No Hertz, listen! I saw him! You can't see your*self*!"

"You can if you're crazy," replied the worm.

Clancy felt a sudden impatience. He normally did not mind Hertz's automatic tendency to question his faith. But something in the word 'crazy' stung this time. He brought back to his mind's eye the image of the other rat, bold, intense, aggressive yet restrained, and supremely self-possessed—in fact, fearless. Apart from the fact that it was clearly, like himself and Aunt

November, a member of the species *rattus norvegicus*, it was totally unfamiliar. Lord, no. That great big rat wasn't him! And besides, that other rat had run off and up into the dumpster, and he, Clancy, was still right here in the churchyard. So Hertz was just being contrary.

"Oh, Hertz," he said. "You know that's not right. Besides, there's no way in the world I could ever have tackled that cat. No, there's another rat in the neighborhood, and I just can't believe it! Lord, I wonder what Aunt November would think!" And for a moment Clancy was lost in reverie, imagining the consternation that his dear old great aunt would have expressed had she ever dreamed that she and Clancy were not the only rats in the vicinity. He did not think for a minute that she would be pleased. She had a low opinion generally of their extended family, and an even lower opinion of most of the members of the family younger than herself. She had been a creature of very exacting standards of deportment, which is why they'd left the squalor of the waterfront in the first place. She wanted stability and order for herself and the nephew whose innocence she was determined to preserve.

Clancy wrested himself out of this reverie and regarded Hertz, who was wriggling his way back to the composter. "I'll talk to you later, Hertz," he said. "I'm going to welcome our new neighbor to St. Aloysius Jr."

❦

HERTZ THE WORM, once safely back in his colony, amongst his numerous and for the most part anonymous progeny, felt unusually reflective. In spite of himself and his commitment to reason, he was intrigued. Had that crazy rat really been rescued? Or was he seeing things? Hertz knew with a weary certainly that, one rat or two, it didn't really matter. Clancy was on another one of his missions.

OFF CLANCY BOUNDED, bold as brass under the open afternoon sky, without a thought of danger. God was obviously watching over him. It was his anointing, after all, to reach out to the dispossessed. He came to the edge of the base of the dumpster, and took as deep a breath as he could manage of the air that was heavy with the stench of hot metal, rotting food, and animal droppings. "Hello!" he cried with ringing tones. "This is Clancy! I believe you just saved my life! I don't know how in the world I can thank you! But I'd love to invite you to join our church! We're not big, and we're not fancy, but we love Jesus, *and* we love visitors. I know you must be a good person, because it's not every rat that would lay down his life for a stranger. I hope you'll join us next Sunday. God bless you, hear?!"

Clancy waited, pricking up his ears to catch any response from within the dumpster, but there was nothing, not even a squeak. Had Hertz been right? Had he merely seen himself? But that was impossible. He wasn't that big and strong. And not that brave, not by a mile. There had to be another rat, and that's all there was to it. It was just going to take some time to reach him.

"You're probably resting," Clancy called after a moment. "Or maybe you're like Hertz, and you need your alone time. I'll let you be. Maybe I'll stop by again tomorrow. Have a blessed day. And thank you for saving me!"

And with that, his duty done, the seed sown, Clancy went back to his basement, for a festive if solitary Sunday lunch.

❧ 2 ❧

EXTREME UNCTION

"Interesting," remarked Ottoline. "So, the young human didn't die after all? He was still alive?"

"Oh no!" said Clancy. At the last Sunday Service he'd announced that he'd be offering a short series of lectures on basic Christian doctrine beside the composter every Tuesday afternoon for the next few weeks, but so far only the pigeon couple, Ottoline and Steven, had made the time to attend. "No, He really did die! But He came right back to life, you see...that's how we know He was the Son of God! See, God made the world, you know, and everyone in it...you, me, and everybody...and when God loves you...and God loves everybody, or He wouldn't have made us...then of course, He doesn't want you to die! He wants us to be around forever and ever! So, he sent His Son, to live and die just like us, to show us that we can live again if we believe! But I guess you have to know that Jesus is the Son of God to believe it. But He was, and that's why I started this Church, to let everyone know that God loves all of us, not just humans, so we don't have to worry about dying!"

"Oh my," Said Ottoline. "Well, that is good news, isn't it, Steven?"

Her mate, a taciturn but agreeable sort, bobbed his head.

"And when did all of this happen, did you say?" Ottoline always liked precision.

"Well, I'm not sure about that..." hedged Clancy. "But I know it was a long time ago. It was long before my Aunt November was born, and you know she lived to be pretty old. And she grew up in the cellar of the same church her grandfather was born in, so that makes it even older..."

"Odd that we're just now hearing about it," said the pigeon. "But perhaps we haven't been paying attention. At any rate, I think it's just lovely. I've always wondered what happens to us after we die, and now I know! We just come back to life, like your Jesus! And, so where is He now, do you have any idea?"

"Oh, He's up in heaven now. He's not on earth anymore...I guess he wasn't too happy about how He was treated. But we can always pray to Him, and He'll help us any way He can! And He'll give us dreams and visions, to let us know what He wants us to do for Him. That's how I know He wanted me to start our church. He told me in a dream..." And Clancy was about to take a deep breath and launch into the story of his own call, when he happened to sense that Ottoline was looking above at the clear blue spring sky. He followed her gaze.

"I don't think Heaven is a place you can see, Ottoline," he said. "Or even fly to, no matter how high you can fly. I think you have to die to get there. And even then, I think you have to be ready."

"Oh," said Ottoline. "Well, I hope it's worth dying for!"

❧❧❧

OTTOLINE AND STEVEN, the pigeons, had already begun to distinguish themselves among the rest of the congregation as being particularly devout and receptive to Clancy's ministry. They never missed a Sunday service, and they were really the only ones who attended Clancy's off-the-cuff but regularly sched-uled catechism sessions, in which he attempted, as best he could, to answer any questions that any parishioner might have about any aspect of the Christian religion. And of course, aside from Clancy, Ottoline and Steven were the only members of the St. Aloysius Jr. Choir.

Having raised several broods, they now quite literally had an empty nest, and had more than enough time and energy and wisdom to give to a fledgling faith community and its pastor. Ottoline, by far the more outgoing of the pair, was particularly eager to approach Clancy with ideas. She seemed to have a knack for spotting opportunities for outreach. Clancy was very quickly beginning to consider her his right paw. Spending time conferring with her in the late afternoons after Grace and Reverend DeBassompierre went home for the day became an essential part of his working day.

"Afternoon, Reverend!" she warbled one breezy Tuesday afternoon. Clancy had just emerged out of the cellar and she fluttered down from her and Steven's favorite spot to perch in the evening, the service line that led from the utility pole beside the driveway to the administrative wing of the church. "I've been waiting to tell you...I had an interesting conversation very early this morning with that lovely opossum, you know, the single mother... I really have to remember to get her name. I believe it's Ometa. Anyway, she was telling me, she enjoys the service so much, and she says your sermons give her so much to think about, but she *is* having a hard time staying awake so late into the morning...she is, after all, nocturnal. She was wondering...and now of course I am too...if it might be possible to have church a little earlier?"

Clancy loved these discussions. He settled into a comfortable crouch and ground his teeth thoughtfully. "Well..." he said. "I suppose we could have a service real early in the morning...but it would have to be real, real early, way before the human service, so that we'd have time for fellowship hour afterward before the people start coming. We don't want to make them think anything's going on, you know. They don't mind you and Steven, but they might get upset if they saw me. The problem is, that might be too early for some of the other members, and to be real honest, it wouldn't be that easy for me...I'm just not an early riser. I wonder, though...I know that one time Reverend DeBassompierre tried to get people to come to a service every Wednesday night...he called it evening prayer. It wasn't exactly the same as the Sunday Service...he didn't even preach...but he said prayers, and the choir sang, and it was real pretty...we could try something like that..."

"That sounds wonderful, Reverend," said Ottoline. "I'm sure she would appreciate it so much. I imagine it does make extra work for you, however?"

"Oh Lord! I'm not worried about that!" cried Clancy. "This doesn't even feel like work to me; it feels like fun! I'd be a pastor all day long if I could! And it's important for us to be as available as we can to our community! You just tell Ms. Opossum that I'll be happy to schedule an evening prayer service any time that she thinks she can make it."

Ottoline agreed and made a mental note to find the opossum first thing, to let her know that her concerns were being addressed. Such was the general tenor of Ottoline and Clancy's informal but regular strategy meetings. Ottoline would present a wrinkle, and together the two creatures, each dedicated in their distinct ways to the growth of the infant church, would smooth the wrinkle out. Over a period of time, Ottoline couldn't help but begin to think of herself as something of an associate minister. She was very clear, however, that she was not called to preach.

AND ALMOST IMPERCEPTIBLY, like any other newborn, the church began to grow increasingly active and adventurous. Ottoline kept an eye out for creatures in the area who seemed as if they would be in search of something more to life. Clancy, taking

St. Aloysius Sr. as his model, experimented with various types of programming. He announced, in fact, right after a fairly well-attended Sunday Service, that he was planning to make himself available on a regular basis as a spiritual director, a ministry that the Reverend DeBassompierre at one time had attempted, without any response, however, from the congregation of St. Aloysius Sr. Still, Clancy thought it would be worth a try.

☙❧

NOT SURPRISINGLY, as with St. Aloysius Sr., the ministry of spiritual direction at St. Aloysius Jr. did not readily get off the ground. No one in the relatively small congregation presented themselves as being interested or in need. Clancy had chosen a spot in the middle of the graveyard, right up against the largest monument there, as suitably private and protected, and as he'd promised, made himself available there on a regular basis for drop-in sessions. But no one dropped in.

He decided to make the most of it by using the time apart for self-examination. As disappointed as he was that no one else seemed willing to explore the working of the Spirit in their lives, he was not going to judge. He reminded himself that what for him was a duty might be for others a luxury. After all, he had the good fortune to be able to live within the church, where his basic needs for food, water and shelter were provided by proximity to humans. He didn't have to work too hard to keep body and soul together, while his parishioners did. Still, often during these solitary hours in the graveyard, nestled in the shade up against the cool marble base of the memorial obelisk for St. Aloysius Sr.'s founding rector, The Right Reverend Bilhaz Withercroft, he found himself wondering aloud, to himself as much as to the Lord, if ministry was meant to be so much fun. After all, many times he'd observed his role model, Reverend DeBassompierre, burying his face in his hands and muttering that if he had to answer one more email or placate one more irate vestry member he was going to go berserk. Clancy, of course, had no email, and no vestry, and so perhaps he was spared at least some of the aggravations of leadership.

In retrospect, Clancy couldn't help but think that God was trying to tell him something, for it was precisely when he was pondering these things in his heart that Ottoline fluttered over, clearly in distress, looking for him. "Oh! Reverend! There you are! Come quick! Oh dear, it's just terrible..."

"Ottoline! What happened!"

Ottoline's rich voice quivered. "Reverend, it's Timmy..."

Clancy's ears burned with chagrin, for he had no idea who Timmy was.

Ottoline perhaps figured as much. "Timmy...the squirrel's youngest. Reverend, he was crossing the boulevard...and he...Reverend, he's been killed." Ottoline took a fluttering jump back, as if to create a distance between herself and the terrible news she'd delivered.

Clancy felt horror suffuse him like a fever. His whiskers stiffened and his impulse was to burrow, to bury himself. Of course he resisted this fleeting temptation, but he couldn't help but reach for his tail and press it to his teeth. When he spoke, it was with a voice muffled by his own flesh. "He's dead?"

"Yes," said Ottoline. "Squashed flat."

Clancy bit his tail. He had to, otherwise he might faint.

Ottoline knew that the Reverend was in shock, but there was no time to lose. "Reverend, his parents are at the curb. They're...they're...I can't even describe it. I'm worried they might...you see, Timmy's still there in the street, and those awful cars keep coming and coming, and some them just...Reverend, I'm afraid his mother might ...please come quickly..."

Clancy's grip on his tail tightened, then relaxed, and he no longer felt faint. He wasn't conscious of making any decision. It was as if something within him took over, asserting itself without displacing his very strong awareness that he had no idea what he was supposed to do. "Okay," he said, and left the shelter of the gravestone and loped across the churchyard, following Ottoline in her low flight to the curb of the deadly boulevard, where two adult squirrels crouched side by side, not touching, as if on the verge of leaping into the maelstrom of traffic. As he drew near to them, with Ottoline just ahead, he heard, louder and closer than ever before in his life, the swift relentless noise of the automobiles as they sped past, and felt and smelled the cloying heat of all the exhaust. He was aware as never before of the precariousness of life. Once again the impulse to flee and hide was strong. But his sense of duty prevailed. He followed underneath Ottoline's lead to the curb.

"I brought the Reverend," Ottoline murmured. "He's right here."

There was no response from the two squirrels.

And here the cool, automatic determination that had over-ridden the rat's timidity melted away like frost, and he knew that he was really on his own now.

"What am I supposed to do, Lord?" he pleaded silently, but he knew even as he pleaded that there was not going to be any answer. "I'm sorry," he managed to squeak.

Again, no response. Just an unnatural stillness in the face of the seemingly endless stream of vehicles that sped mercilessly before them on the boulevard. Clancy felt inadequate as never before. He himself couldn't conceive of what the parents of a dead offspring must be experiencing.

Of course, he was not unacquainted with sorrow. After all, he had awakened one morning not that long ago to discover his beloved Aunt November dead as a doornail on the pallet of discarded vestments upon which she slept. He'd been shocked, of course, and saddened, and also ashamed, for there had been a tinge of relief within the sadness, for his beloved Aunt could sometimes be a handful. But his Aunt November's death, as surprising as it had been, was not tragic. She'd led a full life, long and exemplary and filled with the struggle and satisfaction of raising him. The death of Timmy was a nightmare in the middle of a sunny afternoon.

Clancy forced himself to look into the boulevard. He knew that what he would see there would never leave him, and would change him, in a certain sense undo him, and very likely haunt him, but he also knew that he couldn't avoid it and continue to consider himself a pastor. He swallowed hard and lifted his gaze, and there, a few yards before him, a bushy upright tail fluttered with a macabre airiness in the wake of passing cars. Attached to this heartless motion was the flattened body of a young brown squirrel. Only the tail remained unmashed on the dark asphalt. Clancy had never seen anything so terrible in his entire life.

Then he turned his head to regard the mother squirrel beside him. She was still as a rock, and her expression was so empty and yet so implacable that Clancy was reminded of that cat. But he knew that Ottoline's concern—that this mother squirrel was determined to retrieve the body of her dead son regardless of the danger to herself—was warranted. He had to do something. "We'll come back," he said in a voice he hardly recognized as his own. "We'll come back later, when there aren't so many cars, and get him. But we have to get away from here now, before someone else gets hurt."

Both squirrels, mother and father, looked at him. He regarded them both with all of the steadiness he could feign. He knew he was in grave danger of alienating them from himself and from the church and possibly from God forever, urging them away from their son, but he also knew he was right. For a long, long time he crouched beside them, determined not to back down.

The father was the first to respond. His head lowered, and he stepped backward, just a step, from the boulevard. "Mildy," he said to his wife, "come on."

He stepped to the side, and his side touched hers, and even within her stillness she seemed to freeze again, before her head began, very slowly, to turn towards her mate. The father squirrel turned, and she followed, and then they both, along with Clancy and Ottoline, began to make their way back to the churchyard.

۞

BACK AT THE familiar site of the composter, Clancy felt in his bones that he'd somehow managed to do the right thing, leading the poor squirrels away from the sight of their crushed son. But now that a bit of the shock was wearing off he had no idea what to say or do next. The mother squirrel soon grew agitated, and the father squirrel could not calm her. "Why?!" she demanded of her mate, then Ottoline, then Clancy. "Why?! He was just trying to cross the *street!* Why don't they ever watch where they're going! My SON!" And she began to run back around the corner of the building towards the boulevard.

The father squirrel, rousing himself from his state of sad torpidity, leaped forward and headed her off, and corralled her back to the composter where Clancy and Ottoline stood speechless and horrified. Clancy held his own tail in his front paws, twisting the end painfully, but the pain did not register—at least not until much later that evening. He observed the father squirrel restraining his dead child's mother with weary strength and hopeless patience.

"We're going home, Mildy. I'm not going to have you getting killed."

"I'm not leaving him in the street like that!" she screamed. "I won't! I won't!"

"Mildy," he said, "he's gone."

She turned on him then with such fury that Clancy, though frozen, his tail in his front paws, cried out. The two squirrels looked at him.

"I'll get him," said Clancy. "I'm going to get him off the street. When the traffic slows down. It won't be long. I promise. Go home and try to rest. I'll take care of..." Clancy was horrified to find that he could not for the life of him recall the young squirrel's name, if in fact he'd ever known it. "I'm so sorry..." he began.

"Tim," said the mother squirrel, and her voice was even, resigned, empty. "Timmy." And with that she allowed her mate to lead her out of the churchyard and into the woods.

❦

CLANCY HAD no idea how he was going to get the little squirrel's corpse off the road, or what he was going to do with it once he had it, but he knew now that he had to see this through. For all he knew the squirrels and their many relations were going to be watching his every move from on high. " Oh Lord," he said to Ottoline, who stood right by his side, "this is awful." He was very grateful for the pigeon's steady presence. "I don't know what to do." He immediately felt ashamed for sounding so unprofessional. But if Ottoline held any judgment, she kept it to herself, merely cooing sympathetically. It was well past sundown, with only an edge of sunlight at the western edge of the world, and Clancy and Ottoline were under one of the shrubs along the gravel driveway of St. Aloysius Sr., watching the traffic on the boulevard dwindle. Eventually the slim light in the west disappeared completely, and a vehicle ran over Timmy afresh every minute or so, and then every couple of minutes, until Clancy knew he could no longer put off the unpleasant task of retrieving the body.

Oh Lord, he said to himself. He reached again for his own tail, and twisted its end, as nervous as a cat. He did not even want to get near that flattened, mangled little body, much less touch it, but he'd made a promise, and as a minister, his promise was also God's promise, wasn't it? To Ottoline he said, "I'm going in. Pray for me."

"I'm going with you, Reverend," said the pigeon. "Now, no argument. I'll be on the line, right over your head, perfectly safe, and I'll be able to warn you as soon as I see a car coming."

Clancy was so glad to hear this he couldn't speak.

Off he dashed, across the rather gravelly-grassy front lawn of the churchyard, to the now cool cement curb. There, just a yard or so before him, lay what remained of poor Timmy. Now even his bushy tail was flattened against the asphalt, as if it, too, had given up the ghost. Clancy glanced up, and sure enough, Ottoline was perched directly above him on the thick black power line, still and reassuring. Clancy took a deep breath and looked both ways. No vehicles in sight. He hopped out onto the asphalt, and crouched next to Timmy.

As it turned out, to Clancy's intermingled relief and disgust, getting Timmy off the street was not too difficult; the flattened corpse was not the least bit heavy. It was more a matter of peeling than lifting. Starting at the tail, Clancy tugged, encountered only slight resistance, so then with his own front claws he pried the crushed abdomen, trailing strands of flattened entrails, off of the rapidly cooling surface of the boulevard. As the rat peeled it up, Timmy's body made a sticky noise that turned Clancy's normally strong stomach, but he swallowed his gorge and kept on. The crushed head, with its lolling flat tongue, was the hardest to deal with. Clancy did not want to leave any trace of Timmy on that busy thoroughfare, so he worked with relative slowness, even using one claw to pry Timmy's flat tongue off the street. Even after all that, a dark smudge remained around the place where Timmy's head had been, and Clancy did not want to imagine what the stain might be the residue of. Holding Timmy's flat but basically intact form across his back, he bounded back to the shrubbery. Ottoline flew behind at a respectful distance.

He crept around the building and into the graveyard, where he finally shrugged off his loathsome burden. He thought it would be best and most fitting to leave the poor corpse for the time being in the shelter of that grandest monument among the more humble tombstones and markers, the marble crypt, sealed for eternity, in which reposed the remains of the very first rector of St. Aloysius, The Right Reverend Bilhaz Withercroft, 1894-

1971, a Freemason. Clancy laid the flat little form out right up against the base of that monument and backed away. He was suddenly so exhausted that he wondered if he could even make it back to the basement. There was nothing more he could do in this sad situation. He put his front paws together, bowed his snout, and said a prayer for the repose of Timmy's soul. Then he looked up at Ottoline, perched upon the top of the crypt, and opened his mouth to say that he was going to go home to rest, when he saw just overhead, a circling shadow in the clear moonlit sky above them.

What in the world, he said to himself. Ottoline looked up herself, and burbled her annoyance. "Oh poo," she cried. "A buzzard! They are so heartless! Absolutely no manners whatsoever..."

Clancy's little heart sank. The pigeon was right. The grotesque descending, revolving shadow was indeed a buzzard, just biding its time until the poor corpse of Timmy was left unattended. Clancy knew he was not going to receive the comfort of his own pallet that night. He was going to have to safeguard, as best he could, poor Timmy, so that his mother and father would know that he had kept his promise and watched over what was left of their beloved son. A pastor's work was never done.

৩৩

"You better go on back to your nest, Ottoline." Clancy tried to sound hearty. "I'm sure Steven's wondering where you are..."

"What are you going to do?" asked the worried pigeon.

"I'll have to stay here with the...with Timmy," said Clancy. "And make sure nothing happens to him." He couldn't stop glancing nervously up at the steadily descending shadow. But he didn't want Ottoline to think he was not up to this. "I don't mind," he said. "It'll give me time to pray. And maybe think about putting together a service..."

Ottoline wanted nothing more than the quiet, steady presence of her beloved mate, but she knew the Reverend must feel just as sad and weary as she did. He was only nonhuman, after all. "Reverend, are you sure? You aren't used to being outdoors at night..." She indicated the shadow of the buzzard. "We'll watch over Timmy," she said. "We'll take turns. It's better than you being out here by yourself all night."

Clancy was tempted. Ottoline's suggestion made sense. But it just did not feel right and proper. He, after all, was the pastor. Keeping his flock safe...dead or alive...was his responsibility.

"No, Ottoline," he said, "please get some rest. I have to do this."

Ottoline, having raised several broods, knew a declaration of independence when she heard one. "All right, Reverend," she said. "Be careful."

"I will," said the rodent, resisting the impulse to glance up at the sky.

꧁꧂

So Clancy, very aware of how exposed he was, as well as poor dead Timmy, huddled against the side of the Crypt of Bilhaz Withercroft, keeping his eye on the moonlit and starry night sky and the dark circling shadow it held. "Oh Lord," he prayed. "Don't let me fall asleep no matter what you do. I'm used to being up late, but not all night long, so please make that old buzzard fly away sometime soon. Or maybe, Lord, you can help me figure out somewhere I can put Timmy so that nothing can get to him? I guess I could take Timmy back with me to the basement, but he's already starting to smell so bad...No, the only way I can get through this is to stay here in a vigil until his mom and dad have had some rest. Oh well. I guess it's all part of being a Christian.... I just wish it wasn't so chilly...And I haven't had a thing to eat since this morning..."

Clancy wished he hadn't thought about food. For, having thought about it, he remembered that he'd pilfered the discarded half of a little Debbie snack cake out of the waste-basket beside Grace's desk in the administrative wing just that very afternoon, and it was waiting for him in the cellar, just beside his makeshift bed of old choir robes. He could practically smell it...the enticing, irresistible aroma of refined sugar and corn syrup...he felt his mouth begin to water...

So preoccupied was he with his special treat, which would have grown hard and stale by that time, that he did not pay as close attention as he might have to the sky, and the circling shadow gradually descending from it. The shadow grew larger as it grew nearer, and when he caught a whiff of something displacing the phantom sweetness of the Little Debbie—it was the most acrid, stifling stench, like that of the dumpster in the noonday sun—Clancy realized that the shadow was on the ground before him several yards away, and had become flesh, in the form of an enormous, ungainly, scowling, skin-headed, long-necked buzzard.

"Help!" squealed Clancy; to whom, and to what end, he did not know. The large, malodorous, sinister-looking figure before him did not appear to be aggressive; it maintained a considerable distance, and yet Clancy was terrified. What a revolting smell! And that blistered-looking, hook-beaked face! Never before had he seen such an unattractive living being. It looked as if it had been partly plucked or shaved, its neck was so long and bare. The feathers of its wide, long, heavy-looking abdomen were a dull black, and its bright orange legs and feet were gleaming in the moonlight with some thin, glossy layer of a substance that looked sticky. The buzzard gazed right at Clancy with beady black eyes rimmed in sunken bloodshot flesh above that hooked and pointed yellowish beak and said:

"Are you going to eat that?"

Clancy screeched, "Do *what?*"

The buzzard raised its voice. "I said, are you going to eat that? I noticed you've just been kind of looking at it, and I figured when you got it off the road you wanted it for yourself, but it's been a while now, and it's getting kind of late, and you haven't really touched it, so I just figured I'd come down and ask, because I'm real hungry and there's not much else around to eat tonight." And the big buzzard, its features cast by nature into a permanent glower, managed somehow with his bright black eyes and easy tone to convey a kind of affability. It cocked its head jauntily to the left.

Clancy was thunderstruck, first of all by the discrepancy between the creature's macabre, malevolent appearance and its friendly manner, and also by the outrageousness and nerve of its request. He thanked the Lord that Timmy's parents weren't there to hear it!

"I'm sorry," he began. "But this is... You can't..."

Clancy glanced over at poor Timmy's flattened lifeless form, and back at the strange and awful and eager yet utterly unimposing form of the buzzard, so very full of life. Of course he knew buzzards lived off of fresh roadkill, but the ethical and theological implications of this practice had never occurred to him. He wondered if the Lord was testing him.

The buzzard waited quietly for Clancy to go on. He had a remarkable quality of trusting incomprehension, which reminded Clancy of the attitude of many of the congregants of St. Aloysius Sr. as they listened to Reverend DeBassompierre's erudite sermons. Clancy felt his unease and discombobulation recede, perhaps foolishly. The buzzard was offensive to the eye and nose, and his request was inappropriate in the extreme, but he didn't seem to mean any harm or disrespect.

"I'm sorry," Clancy said again, "but...oh dear...I know that you don't know any better, but I am the pastor, you see, of a worshipping community here in this neighborhood, and this poor young squirrel is...was... the son of two of our members. He was hit by one of these awful cars this afternoon, and of course his mother and father are very upset. And I promised them that I would bring him in out of the street and I'm going to offer them a funeral service tomorrow. I don't know what they plan to do with his...remains after that, but ... I don't mean to be rude...but I am sure they don't want anything to eat him." Clancy paused.

The buzzard seemed to be glaring at him, but it was hard to tell.

"Anyway," Clancy trailed on, "I can't let you have him. I hope you understand?"

The buzzard blinked, then blinked again. He—for it was a male buzzard—heard what the rat was saying and marveled afresh at the wastefulness of so many creatures of the land and air. Why did they want to let a perfectly good carcass go to waste? Why, it was such good eating, squirrel, if a little stringy...it was too bad."I understand," he said. "You've got dibs. Well, sorry to bother you. I just thought I'd ask."

Clancy was further disarmed by such agreeableness. "Oh it's no bother," he said. "It's just that...well, I'm pretty sure he was their only son..." And Clancy felt a pang of chagrin here, for he realized that in fact he knew next to nothing about the creature he was going to be expected to eulogize in the next day or so. *I'll have to work fast*, he said to himself. He put that concern aside for the time being, though, because it occurred to him that this living creature before him, as unsightly and malodorous as it most certainly was, was nonetheless a child of the Living God, and more than likely in need of Salvation. And besides, the fellow seemed nice.

"I'm Reverend Clancy," said Clancy. "What's your name, friend?"

"Bertram," said the buzzard. "My family calls me Bert."

"Do you live around here?" Asked Clancy.

"I guess so."

"Well, I'd like to invite you to visit our church," said Clancy with real enthusiasm.

What the buzzard named Bertram really wanted at the moment was to move on if the strange but friendly rat was not going to let him have what was left of the little dead squirrel. But it was in his nature to be agreeable.

"Sure," he said.

"Oh good!" cried Clancy. "We have services every Sunday at ten o'clock in the morning, after all the humans are out of their cars and inside the big church over there. We don't want them seeing us, because they wouldn't understand, so we start our service after they go into theirs. We all sing, and I preach a sermon, and then there's fellowship, where you can just get to know us. I hope to start a Sunday school before long, and of course I'm available any time if you need anything like counseling or spiritual direction. Just let me know! And feel free to bring your friends and family. We welcome everybody!"

Bertram, who came from a large, contentious, and tight-knit family, took note. "Okay," he said. Speaking of family reminded him that he had a hunt to continue, for he had mouths to feed, having his parents, his grandmother, and three younger sisters to provide for. "Well, it's been nice talking to you, but I better get a move on."

"See you Sunday!" said Clancy. "Around ten! God bless you!"

The young buzzard took off with a leap and a great flapping of his wings, leaving behind a fading stench and a heartened Clancy, who, fortified by having won a soul, managed to keep awake through the night to guard the stiffening remains of poor Timmy until the sun rose and Ottoline and Steve came to keep vigil for him so he could get some sleep and have at least a bite or two of his little Debbie snack cake.

🍂

BERTRAM, high up in his roost deep in the woods, was telling his father about the encounter he'd had with the rat before he'd gone on to discover the carcass of a young deer along the interstate. His father, not unexpectedly, was alarmed and not a little angry regarding the interaction with the rat. "Say what now?!"

the elder buzzard cried in his throaty, gurgling voice. "You *talked* to it?!"

"I did, Daddy," said Bertram. "I didn't see that it would hurt. I mean, he was just standing there with that dead squirrel, and he didn't look like he was gonna do anything with it...And, he was real nice...he said he was waiting for the squirrel's folks to come get him, he said he didn't mean to be rude, but he couldn't let me eat him. He wasn't mad or anything..."

"Bert." Bertram's father lifted his bald, rather mottled pinkish head on his long, thin, and equally featherless neck to assert his stature over his rapidly growing, in fact nearly grown son. "I raised you to have more sense. You know good and well you can't trust none of them like that. I don't care how nice they might be to your face, they don't like us, and they never have. They think we're nasty, just because we clean up after them! Now, Bert, you do something like that again and you know what I'll have to do."

"I know, Pa." Bertram felt at once frustrated and sincerely contrite. He understood his daddy's concern, and he also knew that his daddy was getting agitated, and so the best thing to do would be just to keep his beak shut. It was all just too bad. He knew as well as anyone how he and his family and his species were perceived. But he couldn't help but think that there were some nice creatures out there. And he trusted his gut, which, after all, never let him down. And his gut told him that the rat was different. After all, it had invited him to visit church, whatever that meant. Not for the first time, Bertram figured that his father was being too harsh. But he'd get nowhere by arguing.

"Don't worry, Daddy," he said. "I'll do better."

"Good boy," said the elder buzzard, and his long neck relaxed. "Don't push your luck, son. After all, you're the main pervider, now that yer old man's slowing down. Well, come on, son, and let's see what you did get on your rounds today..." And Bertram followed his father's short flight a few limbs down the pine to the main roost where his mother and grandmother and sisters waited. Bertram regurgitated up what remained of the deer and ate it afresh, sharing, of course, with his family the warm, partially digested meat.

⚜

CLANCY FELT it was a good thing that this was not his first funeral...after all, he'd held one for his Aunt November after she went to be with Jesus. On top of that, he'd eagerly observed as Reverend DeBassompierre lay several old parishioners to rest, so he knew the order of service by heart. Nevertheless, he was very nervous. This was not like those other funerals. This was a tragic farewell.

Had he been less nervous, he might have been impressed by the turnout, not just of his regular congregation, but also by visitors. Squirrels came from near and far to view the body and offer chittering condolences to Timmy's mother and father. Ottoline and Steven were there as well, and Hertz, curious and sympathetic in spite of himself, wriggled out of the compost heap and coiled himself unobtrusively on the edge of the garden bed. The service proper opened with a hymn, sung by Clancy and Ottoline and Steven, one of the few that Clancy knew word for word and was able to lead. The hymn was *How Great Thou Art*. And after the hymn came the hardest part. The eulogy.

Oh, how Clancy had agonized and struggled over what to say! After all, what *was* there to say about a young creature, gone too soon, whom he'd never spent any real time with? For after all, though they were his parishioners, he had not known Timmy or his family well before tragedy struck. Of course he could say, as the hymn said, that God was great and that Timmy, like all who have died in Christ, was safe in the arms of the everlasting Lord. But he wasn't sure he should say that. He had a feeling Timmy's mother wouldn't appreciate it. And Timmy was a mystery to him. He thought about asking Timmy's parents about their son, but he had not wanted to upset them. So he'd gone to Ottoline, who had told him what she'd heard: that Timmy and his mother had had a very strained relationship of late, and that in fact Timmy's rebelliousness was and had been for some time the talk of the churchyard. Apparently, Timmy had always been charming, willful and reckless, and furthermore, had his indulgent father wrapped around his paw. And it was in fact those qualities that had led to his death. He'd been—against his mother's wishes —attempting to cross the boulevard to visit a group of friends, of whom his mother had deeply disapproved.

Of course this information complicated Clancy's task considerably, and shocked him as well. What in the world! How could a young person be so foolhardy! And for the rascal to lose his life as a result of disobedience...well, Clancy couldn't help but wonder if divine wrath might not be a factor. But he certainly couldn't suggest that in a eulogy. And yet, was it not his responsibility and sacred duty to speak the Word of God even in tragedy? He tossed and turned and gnawed his tail bloody the night before the service, and awoke in the morning with still no idea what to say from the pulpit. In the end, he left it to the Lord. Upon waking up from his fitful half slumber, which had been ridden with vague nightmares of being chased by cats, he'd decided that he would trust God to guide his tongue.

And so, when the last notes of "How Great Thou Art" were carried away on the breeze, he heard himself say, without forethought, "Great isn't the same as good."

Instantly he was aware of consternation within the little gathering. *Oh Lord*, he thought frantically. *What am I saying?* But he went on, trusting in the Lord. "Life isn't always good. Especially at times like this. When someone young, whom we love, has been taken away. But maybe it can still be great. We aren't always good ourselves. But maybe, even though we're not always good, we can still be great. Timmy was a happy young fellow, full of life. He never met a stranger, and everyone who knew him loved to be around him. Even when he was not following the rules. And isn't that great? Jesus tells us that the peacemakers are blessed. And who makes peace better than someone who has high spirits, and who everyone wants to be around?

"Timmy was adventurous. And sometimes that means that you take chances that maybe worry the ones you love. You go places that others wouldn't go. That doesn't make you bad. It makes you different. Jesus was like that, and so were so many of our friends in the Bible, like Abraham and Moses and David the King of Israel.

"Now, I know that many of you don't know those stories...but you knew Timmy. You know that he didn't have an enemy in the world. That he brightened up the day of everybody around him, that he loved his mother and father, and he knew that they loved him so much that he could go anywhere and do anything and not lose their love. That's the kind of love that the Lord has for us...It doesn't try to hold us back, but sets us free, by letting us know that we don't have to be good all the time. The Lord knows—the world is a dangerous place. It has to be, or we wouldn't have to look out for one another. And we wouldn't have friends like Timmy, who inspire us to have courage, and to trust that everything will work out somehow. It's a shame that his mother and father have to suffer so badly now that he's gone. But we are here to help. Amen."

Oh Lord, thought Clancy, *that* was awful!

From the composter/pulpit, he regarded the gathering before him, and forced himself to look at Timmy's mother, who was, as before, betraying nothing of her state of mind. She held herself so still that she seemed as absent as flat, dead, dull-eyed Timmy on the ground in between them, covered with a fallen leaf. Timmy's father was visibly agonized; his somewhat patchy tail twitched and his whiskers drooped. "Let us sing," said Clancy, and he signaled Ottoline and Steven to begin the other hymn he'd chosen, *Onward Christian Soldiers*. After that song, which never failed to lift Clancy's spirits, four squirrels, chosen by Timmy's father from among their countless relatives, scampered up as solemnly as they could, picked Timmy up, leaf and all, and bore him away to the forest's edge. At that, Timmy's mother, as if the removal of her son had somehow broken a spell, leaped forward chattering, and with every claw extended, fell upon Clancy, who toppled backward off the top of the composter.

ॐ

THERE WAS PANDEMONIUM, of course, but it very swiftly passed. As soon as Clancy was off the pulpit and on the ground, Timmy's mother took off, chittering and scolding as if pursued by demons or fleas. She dashed around the corner of the building in the direction of the driveway and beyond that, the boulevard. "No, Mildy!" cried her mate, and he took off after her all the way to the curb where their youngest son had last been seen alive. He pleaded with her, he pulled her by the tail, he pushed and shoved her back onto the grass, but she kept twisting away from him to perch on the curb with her tail in a stiff reversed question mark and her forepaws stretched into claws as if to attack the next vehicle to come along.

"Mildy!" he pleaded. "Stop it. Listen to me. This won't bring him back. Please don't do this, Mildy."

But Mildy wouldn't budge. She was going to cross this road and find the hooligans that had led her son to his death if it killed her. And if it killed her, at least she'd be with her son, if there was any truth to what that crazy rat preached.

ॐ

BERTRAM, circling high above that quadrant of the coastal city where he had the most luck in finding roadkill, took a deep, deep breath. Aah! Midmorning was always a good time to scavenge, as the automobile traffic decreased, and so it was easier and safer to reach the spoils. Bertram, though young, had mouths to feed. He was the primary provider, after all, for his parents, sisters, and his elderly grandmother. His father still scavenged, but not like he used to, and Bertram didn't mind going it alone. He liked being away from the squabbles of the nest. And while the interpersonal aspects of scavenging carcasses could get sticky, he was getting much better about navigating it all. The carcasses themselves did not bother him— nothing, after all, was more delicious than fresh dead flesh. But knowing that he and his family were sustaining themselves on the sadness and loss of life of other creatures did give him pause. Precious few of his meals died of natural causes. And indeed, younger corpses tasted better in general. And of course Bertram knew that just about every other creature despised him along with the rest of his species. Bertram's father had always warned him to stick to his own kind, advice that Bertram generally tried to follow. He'd had many unpleasant encounters with aggrieved and sometimes even confrontational survivors on the scene of a fresh roadkill. He remembered with unease a particularly wounding run-in with a mother opossum over the corpses of a number of her young who had been following her across what was supposed to be a quiet country road. That's why he'd been so surprised by the friendliness of the rat! Never before had another species spoken to him so civilly. And to invite him to whatever his church was! Bertram very much wanted to go. He knew, though, that his family, particularly his father, would be furious if they ever found out. He would have to think about it.

He dipped his left wing, and executed a curve. To his right the vast ocean spread out towards infinity; directly below him was the bustling waterfront of the city. The underlying odor of decomposition rose like a prayer, and he took another deep, refreshing breath, but a descent into the busy waterfront district, especially when it was still daylight, was too risky. He continued to curve before aligning himself over the highway, heading north out of the city all the way past the suburbs. Then he made a sharp left to soar above the marshy expanse of the wetlands that surrounded the city. He was following the faint but increasingly promising scent of a rotting fox that had some time before had a fatal encounter with a Dodge Wrangler. Bertram stuffed himself with this jackpot as full as he could and then navigated southward to his family roost to regurgitate and share the bounty. On the way, stuffed with his delicious burden, he passed over the Church of St. Aloysius, where he saw the small but significant gathering of a variety of living creatures surrounding a rat who was for some reason lying flat on his back in front of a composter. If he wasn't so full and in a hurry to get home he would have descended to see what was going on, and let the rat introduce him. It was at that point that he spied yet another squirrel just in front of the church, and even another one right behind it, the one in front seemingly about to make an attempt to cross the busy thoroughfare. It crossed Bertram's mind that this could mean even more fresh meat before long, for these scatterbrained squirrels never seemed to learn that they shouldn't try to cross four lanes in the daytime.

Daddy'll be real pleased, Bertram thought. He might even come down here himself to get him some squirrel.

Cheered all the more by the thought of so impressing his hard-to-please father, Bertram picked up speed and altitude. From his happy height he saw a tractor-trailer coming, barreling down the boulevard in the squirrel's direction.

The warm, fresh fox meat in his belly turned heavy and sour in his gut. He'd spent his life on the heels of death, but never before had he seen death actually occur. A series of images crossed his mind's eye, the nice rat guarding the dead squirrel; the furious mother opossum hissing and charging him away from her dead babies, and, inexplicably, his father's familiar and perpetual scowl. At the very moment he understood his own sorrow, he saw his chance to prevent at least one occasion of sorrow for another. Without another thought, he circled, dove, and landed with wings outstretched directly in front of Timmy's mother. Then he regurgitated all over her the half-digested remains of the precious fox. Thoroughly blocked by the buzzard's wingspan, temporarily blinded by the gastric acidic

filth he'd spewed, she fell backward and well out of the path of
the speeding tractor trailer, which listed so close to the curbside
that the very tips of Bertram's tail feathers were not unpainlessly
crushed. She chittered furiously, swiping her paws across her
eyes as she was dragged by the other squirrel to the gathering at
the composter around the back of the church. Bertram followed.

❦

"REVEREND!" cried Ottoline! "Oh my stars! She's been hurt!
She's bleeding!"

Clancy had been trying to slip away back to his cellar when
he heard Ottoline's cry. He scrambled back to her side, and his
little dark eyes popped at the sight of Timmy's mother, covered
with gore, being dragged along by her mate and followed by...of
all creatures...the very same young buzzard that had asked
permission to consume Timmy! Clancy shrieked and dashed
towards this extraordinary procession.

"Oh Lord!" he cried. "What happened!" Timmy's mother was
a ghastly sight, all pulpy flesh and matted fur, and she kept
rubbing at her face, which, though intact, was covered with the
same kind of viscous slime that he'd noticed on the legs and feet
of the buzzard the night of the vigil. And she smelled atrocious.
"Oh God! Oh Jesus! Please don't let her die!" And as if he imagined he could retain her spirit by making contact with her flesh,
disgusting though it was, he fell forward and his snout touched
hers.

She reared back as if electrocuted. "Get away from me!" she
shrieked, and, breaking out of her mate's gentle grip, she took off
blindly in the direction of the woods. Her mate, Timmy's father,
who's name was Elwood, called out for her, but did not follow.
He watched until she was nothing but a rustling of leaves up in
the boughs of a sugar maple at the edge of the playground. "She's
gone home," he said. He turned to the buzzard. "You saved her."

"What?" cried Clancy with real puzzlement, even though he

was the one who had just begged the Lord to preserve her. But his puzzlement turned into awe. It looked as though He had.

Elwood addressed the young buzzard as if Clancy were not there. "I couldn't stop her...but you did. Mildy'd be gone if it wasn't for you. And I would be too." Timmy's father blinked and blinked, like someone waking up from a very deep and bewildering dream. He looked over at Clancy, as if for an explanation. But Clancy could only reach for his tail and bend the tip of it this way and that in his front paws, captive in his consternation to this nervous habit.

"Can't be too careful crossing the street!" said the buzzard. "Those daggum cars don't stop for nobody, believe me."

"I know," said Elwood sadly, and then he crawled off to the woods. Clancy regarded the buzzard before him with awe and wonder. "How...?" he began. "What...?"

"Buzzard puke," said Bertram, as if that explained everything. But seeing the Reverend's confusion, he went on. "That's how we stop anyone trying to come for us. I can aim so good I can hit a copperhead in the eye. First thing my daddy ever taught me," he added. "We have to look out for ourselves."

"You vomited on Mildy?" said Ottoline, who had come to stand beside the Reverend, doing her best to overcome her aversion to the sight and smell of the great big buzzard.

Bertram regarded the pigeon, a type of bird that his father had always dismissed as 'snooty, for all that they're common as dirt.' She certainly sounded pretty stuck up. He waited before he answered.

"I guess I did. Maybe you would have thought of something better."

"I doubt that very much," said Ottoline. "You are certainly very resourceful. Reverend..." she said, turning to Clancy, "I think we should invite this very brave young person to join us for worship this Sunday."

"Oh, he already asked me," said the buzzard, mollified by her graciousness. "And I can't wait."

"YOU KNOW," said Bertram to Ottoline following the next Sunday service, "I've been told by some that I can carry a tune."

Ottoline looked at him in some surprise. Judging by his very peculiar, distinctive, gargly and rather rustic speaking voice, it was hard for her to imagine that the buzzard could sing. "Is that right?" she said.

He nodded.

It was clear to Ottoline what he was getting at. He had approached her, as a matter of fact, just seconds after she and Steven had sung the final notes of the closing hymn. She wasn't sure what the Reverend would think or say, but it seemed to her that there was only one thing to do. "Well, would you like to join our choir?"

"Can I?" croaked the buzzard. "I sure would enjoy it."

Ottoline spotted Clancy some distance away, in what was apparently a deep and pastoral conversation with the mother opossum, whose six young ones clung heavily to her like enormous overstuffed ticks. "We should check with the Reverend first ...as soon as he's free...but I'm sure he would be happy for you to lend your voice to our little choir."

"Okay!" croaked the buzzard, ever agreeable.

❧ 3 ❧

BAPTISM

"**I** don't like it, Bert, I just don't like it ," said Bertram's daddy, shaking his wattled bald head and deepening his perpetual scowl. "And your mama don't like it neither, nor your granny. It's dangerous, don't you understand? Don't go getting mixed up with critters you don't know nothing about."

"But Daddy..." Although Bertram had expected his daddy to be displeased, he was a little surprised at the vehemence of the reaction. He did not like being at sixes and sevens with his family, especially his father, but the fact was that he couldn't help it. He'd been asked by Ottoline to perform at a very important service, and it was going to take a lot of practice and preparation. It meant mastering a hymn of Ottoline's own composition, and it was all very exciting and gratifying. He would love nothing more than for his family—and especially his strict daddy—to share with him the wonderful sense of fellowship and expanded opportunity for spiritual growth that becoming a member of St. Aloysius Jr. had given him. But he knew it was difficult for them to overcome their really very justifiable clannishness.

"Daddy?" Bertram tried to be gentle. "Do you think I'd do anything that would bring us trouble? I promise you, I'm real careful. I just think we've been keeping to ourselves a little too much. And you know what, Daddy, they're all real nice! Even the pigeons... I mean they did seem snooty at first, but I found out that's just their way. Actually, they're real friendly. And the rat...he says that the Lord made us all equal in His sight..."

Betram's daddy hissed. This was his habitual expression of disdain. Then he spat. "Sounds like a load of dookie to me. He's buttering you up for some reason, son, you mark my words. I don't trust them rats for one minute. Not till they're good and dead, and sometimes not even then; they make for mighty tough and greasy meat. Son, I mean it, I don't want you going down there no more."

Bertram knew he was not going to convince his father of anything, especially not in the contentious and combative mood the old buzzard seemed to remain in lately. He decided that the best way forward was to just keep his beak shut about his new life. But it was all so sweet to him that it seemed such a shame not to share it with the ones he loved the most! He decided he'd discuss the whole issue with the Reverend.

৩৫৬

To be assured of their privacy, they took a stroll together up and down the rows of headstones in the church cemetery. With Bertram beside him, so large and formidable in appearance, Clancy felt very safe.

"Reverend, my daddy...really my whole family...doesn't want me coming over here and being with you all," gargled Bertram bluntly and sadly. "And I don't want to go against them, but I feel like it's not fair. It's all right for them to keep to themselves, they don't mind it, but I have always liked to talk to different creatures. I think we're all the same, deep down. But my family, especially my daddy, doesn't think anyone else likes us..." And Bertram came to a stop, in the shadow of the great monument to the memory of Reverend Bilhaz Withercroft, and spread his wings just a little bit in a gesture of resignation.

Clancy could certainly relate to his new parishioner—and friend's—dilemma, and was eager to do so. "Oh, I know just how you feel! My Aunt November was the exact same way. She was a wonderful aunt, don't get me wrong, and a good Christian rodent, but she did not have a trusting spirit. I think it was because of her upbringing. She lost her own mama when she was real young and had to move from a little church cellar out in the country to the waterfront, where she didn't understand their ways, and she felt like all her brothers and sisters and their children...including *my* mama...were living wrong, and acting trashy, so she rescued me from all that and we came here...and I praise the Lord every day that I was brought up in the Church. But still, Aunt November wanted us to just stay to ourselves, and I really didn't go outside the church at all and I didn't make any friends—unless you count Reverend DeBassompierre—until Aunt November went to be with the Lord and Hertz came along, and that just seemed like a miracle to me, because I was getting pretty lonesome..."

Bertram listened, and though he found Clancy's attempt to relate encouraging, at the same time his own distress was steadily building, because his conflict was, after all, very immediate. After a while he just could not contain himself, and he burst out with a great, irrepressible croak. "Why can't we all be friends!" And Clancy, who could not be insensitive to the deep anguish of the young buzzard, fell silent and shifted his attention away from his own past.

Bertram apologized. His daddy would have swatted him had he ever interrupted *him* like that! But the rodent did not seem to mind. Bertram lowered both his voice and his head. "I guess I'm pretty upset. I've always felt like my daddy knows best, but lately he's been more and more grouchy, and sometimes I feel like he just doesn't love me no more..." And with that, the strength seemed to drain from the young buzzard's long and sturdy neck, and his head hung so that he was the very picture of dejection.

It was enough to break Clancy's tender heart. "Oh, that can't be true, Bertram. I know your daddy loves you very much, just like my Aunt November loved me. She just wasn't the type to show it. Listen, if you think it'll help, I'll be happy to talk to your daddy. I'm sure if he sees how diverse we all are here at St. Aloysius Jr., he'll understand that we love everybody! We love him, too! Maybe you can ask him to come in for some counseling."

Bertram could not imagine his father agreeing to take counsel from anyone, much less a non-buzzard, and said as much to Clancy.

"Well..." Clancy reached for his tail and twisted it while he pondered. "Maybe if he just visited one of our services, he'd see that we don't judge?"

Bertram didn't think that attending a service would cause his daddy to feel anything except scorn, but at the same time he hated to discourage his nice new friend. And if what the rat believed about the god of the humans was true, then miracles could happen. He lifted his head a bit. "Maybe," he allowed.

"I know!" shrieked Clancy, suddenly inspired. "I know! What we need to do is have a service that'll show him just how much we love you and want you to be a part of our church! We'll have a formal service to welcome you..." Clancy then had an idea that struck him as being so perfect and so inspired by the Holy Ghost that he dropped his tail and raised his front paws above his snout in a gesture of utter and absolute exultation. "That's it! We'll baptize you! Oh, praise the Lord! It's perfect! It's just what the church needs, especially after what happened to poor Timmy..."

Clancy's beady black eyes bulged and brightened with excitement. He felt as if the entire universe had suddenly become exponentially larger, as if he himself might explode with happiness.

Bertram didn't share the rodent's elation, and as he did not even know what a baptism was, he couldn't imagine his family taking any pleasure or interest in it. Still, he supposed it wouldn't hurt to ask them to attend.

"I'll see if I can get them to come, Reverend," he said. "But what's baptizing?"

ॐ

CLANCY RETURNED to what he was quickly coming to consider his 'office,' his base of operations, that is, the area of the community garden lying closest to the back of the 'mother' church building where the compost bin was placed. He could hardly contain himself for excitement...A baptism in the works! How perfect! It seemed as if every day brought a fresh opportunity for him to be more pastoral. The only thing that bothered him was the fact that he had not thought of baptism beforehand. It seemed obvious to him now that any pastor with a brain would have been baptizing like crazy just as soon as the church got started.

I guess it's just the Lord's will, he said to himself, that I'm a little slow. And of course I've had so much else to worry about...poor Timmy getting killed, and that darn cat...well, it's all working out, because this way Bertram gets to be our very first baptized Christian. And maybe that's because God knows that Bertram's daddy has that suspicious spirit; he needs to see a great big beautiful show of God's love and acceptance. That's why this is going to be the best baptism ever...

Then Clancy imagined the upcoming ceremony: Bertram's father, experiencing the glorious liturgy and witnessing his son's life-changing entry into the communion of saints, would be emotionally overcome—so overcome that he would offer *himself* for baptism and encourage the rest of the family to do the same. So he was a bit startled when Ottoline appeared before him, having descended with her customary chuckle from the empty ornamental belfry atop St. Aloysius Sr. where she and Steven roosted at night.

"Ottoline!" he exclaimed. "Oh! I'm glad to see you! I just had the best idea! We're going to baptize Bertram!"

"Wonderful!" crooned Ottoline. "But what does baptize mean?"

The question was immediately sobering to Clancy. He had already had to explain to Bertram the nature and purpose of the rite, but now he realized that even his most loyal parishioner had no conception of this most basic Christian ceremony. It brought home just how much work he had yet to do. His elation leveled. It was always humbling to remember that, unlike himself, most poor creatures had been left outside the saving knowledge of Christ through no fault of their own and were starting from scratch. "Oh!" he said. "Wow! I guess I haven't preached on it yet. Baptism is..." He paused.

Ottoline stood, patient though puzzled, as Clancy struggled to articulate, in terms a total novice might be able to comprehend, the mystery of Christian Initiation. "Well..." he began, "I guess you could say, it's like getting cleaned up. It takes away all of your sins, and you start fresh. You get born... or hatched...again." He reached for his tail and held it against the fur on his chest. Something in this totally unconscious and self-soothing gesture brought to him the vague hazy memory of his irresponsible and self-indulgent mother, from whom his Aunt November had rescued him as an infant before he got too attached. "Jesus said we have to be born again, and baptizing is how we do that. We start fresh when we get baptized into the church, because getting baptized makes us clean. We baptize with water that's been blessed, and that means it's holy, and when we're cleaned up with it, then we're holy. So I'm going to baptize Bertram, and he'll be saved. Isn't that great?!"

"It sounds wonderful!" said Ottoline. "And the rest of us?"

Clancy blinked. Ottoline had done it again—thought of something he should have thought of. What *about* the rest of the church, indeed?! Come to think of it, no one in the church, apart from Hertz, that is, had been baptized, and as a matter of fact, he wasn't at all sure that he had access to the water that was needed, or—and here he felt his eyes bulge—he wasn't sure that he himself had been baptized. Aunt November had somehow never mentioned it. But surely she would have seen to his salvation?! He reached for his tail.

"Reverend?" said Ottoline. "Have I spoken out of turn?"

Clancy wrenched his attention away from what he now imagined to be the precarious state of his own soul and back to the matter at hand. "Sorry," he said, his front paws still twisting his tail. It seemed so painful that Ottoline had to look away. "You're right, Ottoline. You always think of everything, don't you! Yes, we need to baptize everyone! Everyone who wants to be baptized, at least. Oh Lord...what would I do without you to let me know what I'm not thinking of? Sometimes I think maybe *you* should be in charge instead of me, Ottoline..."

"Don't be silly," crooned the pigeon. "No one can think of everything. Now, let me get this straight. By everyone, do you mean everyone who attends our Sunday services regularly? Including Steven and myself?"

Clancy stopped twisting his tail end and released it so that it settled comfortably on the ground. He clasped his front paws together and asked, "You and Steven want to be baptized?"

Ottoline's eyes twinkled. "Well, it sounds lovely," she said. "I think I can speak for both Steven and myself, that we would be honored to be included."

Clancy's heart leaped. The pigeon's interest in being formally initiated, while not unexpected, was yet so graceful and sincere that it seemed miraculous. Now he knew he was on the right track.

"I'm so happy I can't stand it!" he enthused.

☙❦❧

"DADDY..." Bertram decided to come right out with it. His daddy, who didn't like much of anything, certainly did not like for Bertram or any of his offspring to beat around the bush. "Daddy... I got something to tell you. I'm going to be baptized!"

The two buzzards sat on two branches of a limb that spread from near the topmost height of the tall dense oak in which they made their multilevel roost. The limb supporting Bertram's father was a bit higher and much thicker.

"Do what, now?" said the old buzzard, who had forgotten that Bertram was nearby.

Bertram had hoped to find his father in a benign after-supper mood, but it looked like that wasn't the case this evening. The older buzzard seemed very preoccupied.

"Are you all right, Daddy?" said Bertram.

"Course I am," snapped the older buzzard sharply.

"Well, you look like you've got something on your mind."

"I ain't got nothing on my mind," said his Daddy. "Least I didn't! Now, what're you going on about?"

Bertram tried not to sound as if he were saying anything that could possibly be disagreeable to his father. "I just wanted to let you know, I've decided to be baptized, Daddy. That means I'm going to join that church. That church that the rat I told you about started. Now, Daddy, I know you don't..."

From somewhere within Bertram's father a low gurgling sound issued.

"Daddy, I promise you, it's nothing that will get in the way of me..."

"No you ain't." The elder buzzard's response was low and even.

Bertram was not surprised by his father's response. He was not prepared, however, for the ominous calmness of it. It was as if his father knew something he didn't know. Still, Bertram knew a thing or two about how to placate the elder buzzard. He drew in his neck and wings and seemed to shrink.

"Now Daddy..." he said. "You know if you're really against it, I won't go against you."

"Durn right."

"But Daddy, don't you think it might be good for us if I see what some of them are like? They might even help us out, if they stop not liking us...and you know, that church is right there on the boulevard, and there's always lots of..."

"Don't matter!" the elder buzzard barked. "I don't need no help perviding for my family, and you shouldn't neither. We're not gonna take help from nobody."

Bertram had heard it all before, and never before had he questioned or reflected upon his father's strict principles of self-reliance and family loyalty. But now he wondered, what was the point of them? They hadn't seemed to make life any easier or happier for the old buzzard. But he clung to them as if to life itself. Bertram became aware, for the first time in his young life, of a growing edge of contempt for his father. He's just an old grouch, he said to himself.

Did the elder buzzard sense this shift in attitude? For his own stench sharpened and strengthened, as if to assert its dominance over the cool evening breeze that was tinged with pine and the not very distant sea. "Bert, I'm not going to hear any more of this mess about that rat and whatever it is he's doing or wanting you to do. Ever since you come across that damn rat you ain't been right. It just goes to show, if you get too close to them when they're living they try to get in your head. See how they're turning you against your own daddy? I reckon I should've known you might be too soft to start scavenging on your own. From now on, I'm coming with you. You hear me?!"

"I hear you, Daddy," said the young buzzard. He hung his head, but he was pleased. He'd hoped his father would come around to precisely this point. He'd get the old buzzard to church one way or another.

"FIRST THINGS FIRST," said Ottoline. "Practical considerations. As you say, we'll need water—unless it rains, and even then there may not be enough. The way I see it, we have two options, and there are positives and negatives associated with each. There's a

creek that winds through the woods all the way to the marsh-
land. It would take some time to get everyone there, and of
course there's some risk, but we would be out of the sight of any
of the humans. Then, on the other wing, there's our bath, over in
front of the big building...but of course there the problem is that
anyone and everyone can see what's going on..."

Clancy had never before paid much attention to the nonde-
script cement birdbath near the gravel driveway of the church.
He glanced over at it now. Of course! Of course! Apart from its
pitted concrete pedestal it even looked a little bit like the admit-
tedly much larger, deeper and altogether more ornate baptismal
font in the sanctuary of St. Aloysius Sr.! Why hadn't he thought
of that! It was perfect. "That's it!" he exclaimed, so suddenly and
with such volume that Ottoline was taken aback.

"But Reverend, like I said, it's so conspicuous. Don't you
think it would be too dangerous? We're sure to attract unwanted
attention."

Clancy deflated. Of course, Ottoline was right, as always.
The birdbath was right out in the open, clearly visible from the
boulevard and the church proper to any nosy human or any
other questionable creature who might happen to be watching.
It was no place for any significant gathering. It was too bad.

"It's a shame we can't have the baptism at night," remarked
Ottoline.

Clancy squealed. Ottoline's feathers stood on end; she was
still not accustomed to the Reverend's bursts of enthusiasm.
"Oh! Lord! I'm sorry, Ottoline! But that's it! There's no reason
why we *can't* have our baptism at night! Half the congregation is
nocturnal anyway, don't you know! Oh Ottoline, you're a genius!
What in the world would I do without you!"

Ottoline demurred. "Shall we plan on this coming Sunday
evening, then?"

"Okay," said Clancy. "That gives us time to let everyone
know, and I'll have time to figure out a sermon. And you and
Steven will sing, won't you, Ottoline?"

"If you like," said Ottoline. "If you think it's fitting."

"Why wouldn't it be fitting?"

"Well, since we'll be taking part in the baptism itself, I just thought maybe it would be awkward if we performed as well, but if you think it's all right ..."

Clancy reined himself in. "Well, if you think it's too much..."

Ottoline couldn't help but chuckle. She, who had raised a dozen broods, overwhelmed by a song! "Don't worry about that, Reverend. You know we enjoy singing..."

In his mind's eye Clancy beheld, in a vague, amorphous, and yet compelling sort of vision: a host of saints and angels into which he and his little flock were being timelessly assumed. And in his mind's ear he could hear, as if silence itself had the capacity to proclaim, an eternal hymn. And with this, the very daylight within which the pigeon and himself stood together took on a fresh dimension. It was as if some invisible veil between the seen and unseen, the heard and unheard, had lifted. Clancy could not contain his delight, but leaped forward and threw his front paws around Ottoline's ringed neck. "Just a few more days, and we'll all be saved! Praise the Lord! And praise you, too, Ottoline!"

NOW THAT THE date and time and place were determined, Ottoline saw to it that the word spread. She, having the advantage of flight and the self-assurance that comes of a decided character, was not timid about putting pressure upon even the most casual of members to take part in or at least attend this most significant service. She even approached Timmy's grieving parents and carefully appealed to them both, suggesting that if they could manage to simply show up, it might do them some good, and would certainly reassure the Reverend. Timmy's father Elwood agreed that it would not hurt, and Timmy's mother Mildy said nothing.

Meanwhile Clancy concentrated on formulating what was, the more he considered it, an extremely delicate ritual. For not only would he be baptizing Bertram and anyone else who might present themselves for baptism, but he was also going to baptize himself, just to make sure. But then the question became, should he go first? Or last? Or in between? What would Jesus do? Oh how he wished he could consult with someone, ideally Reverend DeBassompierre. But it was impossible. Hertz, as usual, though, could be counted on to have an opinion.

"Go first," said the worm. "Why not? After all, you're the boss."

"Oh, Hertz, I'm not the *boss*! The church doesn't have a *boss*. I'm just the pastor, Hertz, that doesn't make me any more important than anybody else! It just means that...well...I'm responsible for preaching the gospel and teaching the bible and reaching the lost, and...showing the way."

"THEN GO FIRST!" cried the exasperated worm.

Clancy let that settle the question.

☙❧

"HOLD ON! Where do you think you're going, Bert!"

Bertram was perched at the end of his favorite branch, his wings outstretched, poised for flight. He'd held that not very comfortable position for some time before his daddy noticed. "It's the dead of night!" the old buzzard said.

"I'm hungry, Daddy," said Bertram. "I was just gonna take a little look around to see if I can find something to snack on."

His father grumbled and hopped onto the limb upon which Bertram was perched, causing it to wobble, then steady. "Don't give me that, Bert," he said. "I may be ignorant, but I'm not dumb. You're up to something. You're off to see that durn Donna I told you to stay away from."

"No, I'm not, Daddy, I promise." And Bertram was hopeful that in the darkness his father couldn't see the pale flesh of his scalp flushing at the mention of the vulture Donna, whose solitary roost was on the other side of town. That attractive female was another point of contention between father and son. "I'm just a little hungry. And I can't sleep. I think I just need to stretch my wings a little. Don't you trust me at all any more, Daddy?"

Bertram's father's stench thickened the air between them. "Not when it comes to that whore," he said. "I don't want you going nowhere tonight."

"But Daddy..." said Bertram. "It's such a good night to be out! It's a Friday! All the people are out in their cars, lots of them young and more of them drunk ...and it's rutting season for the deer! I could find us a real feast tonight, Daddy!"

Bertram's tone became wheedling, which he knew got under his father's skin terribly.

"Quit that whining," said his daddy. "You sound just like your mama."

Bertram hung his head to suggest deference, but kept an eye on his daddy, who he knew was not unpersuaded by the prospect of a good haul. The atmosphere between them gradually softened. "It *is* a wild night out," the elder buzzard admitted. "Might be a good idea to take a look around. All right. But I'm coming with you, you hear?"

"Daddy, you don't have to do that. You need your rest."

"I told you, I'm coming! I ain't so old I can't hold my own! Now let's go, before your mama tries to stop us."

Bertram was pleased by his own cleverness. He spread his wings and was off into the night, with his father right behind him. The night sky was clear and the streets and buildings of the city below them truly didn't appear as dormant as the late hour might suggest. The main roads were active, if not busy, but if there were any casualties Bertram couldn't scent them. And of course the truth was that he didn't really want there to be any feast on the ground this night. He was not lying when he told his father that he was hungry, but his hunger was of course for spiritual food, the sustenance of a supportive faith community. And on top of that, it was time to take a stand.

Oh! It felt fine to be out and about at night, and on his way to something new and different. He could sense his daddy's growing suspicion as they approached the boulevard, and he began to feel something like guilt. He loved the old buzzard, after all, and did not relish the idea of putting one over on him and giving him some real justification for distrusting him. This wasn't the first time, after all, that Bertram's own natural tendency towards gregariousness had caused problems between himself and his sire. There was also Donna, Bertram's first and recent love, a vulture a few seasons older than him, and already with a brood of her own, who had been abandoned by her mate for reasons that remained mysterious. Bertram had made her acquaintance in the course of a scavenging trip, and he'd been instantly smitten. There was just something about her that mesmerized him. She was beautiful, to be sure, with eyes rimmed with the deepest red he'd ever seen, but when he'd mentioned her to his father, he thought the old buzzard would knock him out of the roost. "Vulture!" his daddy spat. "Nothing but one of them stuck-up city buzzards. Think they own the place, just because we came here from out in the country. They're as bad as humans! Don't want to share their finds...You stay away from that hussy, Bert, I mean it. She's laying some kind of trap for you, believe you me. You'll feed her brats over my dead body! Trust and believe!"

Since then Bertram had continued to visit Donna in her lonely exile under the water tank along the causeway, but not without trepidation, because he knew that if his father caught wind, there would be hell to pay. He couldn't help but hope against hope that tonight he could help his daddy see reason. It was, like most things in life, worth a shot.

He now took a deep breath of the briny air high above the coastal city. What, he wondered, not for the first time, was the point of raising a brood, if in the end one didn't allow or want them to have their own friends and families? What did his daddy think would happen if he never allowed any of his offspring to make new acquaintances? Nothing would ever change, nothing new would happen, every day would be the same until—well, eventually, they would all be dead. And then what? What was it all for? Bertram loved his family, his daddy, his mother, his sisters and even his rather querulous granny, but the prospect of remaining with them and only them for the rest of his life—and apparently even beyond—made his heart sink. No, he said in his head as he began an incremental descent towards the church, daddy may never speak to me again, but I can't just do everything he wants. If he wants me to keep helping him, he's got to let me have my say.

As if on cue, his daddy squawked and flapped and shouldered up alongside him. "Bert! Where do you think you're going! There ain't no carcass down there!"

"I'm going to join the church, Daddy," said Bertram as calmly as he could. "You can come with me if you want, but you better be nice to my new friends." And so saying Bertram descended.

❧

THE CEREMONY WAS SET for midnight, for that was the hour at which the boulevard before the church was least traveled, according to Ottoline, who knew the boulevard as well as anyone. By that time of night most of the fast food restaurants and other businesses along the thoroughfare had been shut down for hours, and few if any humans would be anywhere nearby to observe or disturb the proceedings. The plan was to gather at the compost heap at close to that time, and process, with reverence, to the sacred birdbath.

Clancy had promised himself that he would get some sleep before the ceremony, so that he would feel fresh, but the sandman did not visit him that evening, and he tossed and turned for a long time on his pallet of moldering choir robes in the cellar. Finally he gave up on going against his nature and took advantage of the empty church to visit the sanctuary.

The dimness and hush of the sacred space did have a calming effect right away. I should have thought of this before, he told himself; after all, only Jesus can give us true rest. He gazed reverently up at the hanging crucifix and regarded the indistinctly featured face of the suffering Christ beneath His crown of thorns. Lord, he said to himself, I sure hope everything goes the way we planned tonight. And I hope I'm doing the right thing, baptizing myself. If I'm not, Lord, please just let me know... I don't want to do anything that would scandalize Your Name.

From the vast nocturnal silence of the empty sanctuary, the only response seemed to be pure acceptance. Clancy closed his eyes reverently and actually fell into a slumber for a few refreshing minutes. He awakened with a start, having no idea how much time had passed. Oh Lord! he thought. I bet they're all waiting for me!

He scurried out of the sanctuary without his usual farewell genuflection to the crucifix, made his way down to the cellar, and out and around the corner to the composter, where the congregation was set to gather. But no one was there, except for Ottoline and Steven, perched above on the service line that reached from the transformer on the boulevard to the aerial on the roof. "Oh Ottoline!" cried Clancy. "Am I too late? Oh Lord...all I did was close my eyes for one second to pray, and before I knew it I was fast asleep! And I don't know for how long! Oh Lord, did everyone go home?"

Ottoline descended, laughing, from the power line. "It's all right," she said. "There's time. Look at the sky..." She raised her own gaze and they all took in a wonderfully clear and bright starscape. A crescent moon reclined high above, and the effect of it all was to suggest a host of distant and approving spectators. "There's plenty of time," said Ottoline. "Don't worry, Reverend. All is well."

"Oh!" said Clancy, relieved. But where was everybody? Weren't they as excited as he was?

Hertz poked his tip out from within the compost, telling himself he was disturbed by all the squeaking and cooing, but in fact, he was interested. There was no denying that there was something in the air that night, as if anything could happen. "Hertz!" cried Clancy. "Are you going to join us? You sure are welcome, but remember—you've already been baptized. We're not supposed to do it twice..."

"As if I'd want to go through that again," said Hertz. But he emerged completely from the composter, and Clancy was thrilled. He picked up his friend and draped him across the back of his neck like a yoke, the old familiar way the two old friends had of travelling together.

"Oh, praise God," said Clancy ebulliently. He ran around in a little circle.

Ottoline hearkened to something stirring in the night from the direction of the woods. "Reverend," she said. "They're on the way..."

And sure enough, small shadows began to emerge from the outer darkness beyond the glow of the church building's motion sensors.

The squirrels came first, having descended from the trees closest to the churchyard. Mildy and Elwood were among them, bringing up the rear. The enormous mother opossum, with six juvenile opossums clinging to her, whom Clancy had seen in church a few times before, came in from the direction of the dollar store a few blocks down the boulevard from St. Aloysius. Clancy looked at Ottoline, who said that the mother opossum was always looking for things to do to keep her babies occupied. Just as Clancy was beginning to wonder if he should make some formal announcement of welcome, he caught a whiff of that unforgettable odor of decomposition. He looked up, and sure enough, high above but descending steadily in a devolving spiral was Bertram, followed by a form very much like himself.

"There he is! Here comes Bertram! And it looks like he brought his daddy! Oh, praise the Lord!" And Clancy raised himself as high as he could on his hind legs and waved his forepaws.

"Ugh!" Ottoline remarked on perceiving the smell, which made the compost seem refreshing by comparison. As a matter of fact, a quiet revulsion seemed to overcome the whole gathering. Even unflappable Steven averted his beak. It was as if in the midst of a celebration of new life, death was in the air.

But Clancy was as delighted as he could be. "Bertram!" He rushed over to greet his convert. "You made it! And this must be your daddy! Welcome! Welcome! Praise the Lord! I'm Reverend Clancy, of St. Aloysius Jr. Episcopal Church, and I'm just so glad you could join us. Bertram has been such a blessing to us! I just hope you enjoy tonight's service, and that you know you're welcome any time to join us for Sunday services ..."

Ottoline, a parent many times over, couldn't help but sense between the elder and younger buzzards a most discomfiting tension, but she was determined not to be standoffish. She stepped forward and nodded graciously. "Hello, Bertram," she said. "Hello, Mr...."

Bertram's daddy did not even look at her. Ottoline looked at Bertram and did not press the matter. The poor young buzzard was clearly uneasy and embarrassed. She turned to Clancy.

"Reverend, I think it's time..."

Clancy turned to Bertram's daddy, and lowered his snout in the posture of polite deference. "Sir..." he said. "I want you to know, we are an open and affirming community here. Everyone is welcome to worship with us, no matter what their background is or what they eat. We believe that God has made us all the way we are for a reason, and the reason is that He just loves to make life interesting. We don't ask anyone to join us just to tell them later that there's something wrong with them and that they have to change the appetites God made them with. We just want to love Jesus and love our neighbor as ourselves. We love Bertram just the way he is, don't you worry."

The older buzzard's already naturally disgruntled expression seemed to become more fixed. He made a noise deep in his lengthy throat and regarded the squeaking creature before him, who had the nerve to think it could overcome the animosity of countless generations with a little speech like that. "I smell a rat," the old buzzard said, just to be ugly.

"Daddy!" Bertram cried. "Daddy, don't be nasty. The Reverend is just trying to make you feel comfortable."

"I am comfortable," said the old buzzard. "Seems to me *you* ain't, though. You lied to me, Bert. And here I thought I could trust you again. But I ain't stupid. When I saw you about to slip away tonight I knew you weren't up to anything right. I've tried to make a buzzard out of you the best I know how, but you do what you want no matter what, always have, come to think of it. Well, if you want to leave your own family to starve just to suck up to strangers, I can't help that. But I ain't gonna stick around and watch. I got to get my rest. Looks like I'm the one that has to keep the family going now...it's a damn shame, at my age, just when I should be able to take it easy and let the son I raised do for me..."

Clancy couldn't bear for the older buzzard to go away feeling abandoned. He interposed himself between father and son and faced the father with his paws clasped pleadingly.

"Oh, sir..." The elder buzzard glared so that Clancy stepped back, and his prominent testicles drew in as if for safety. "Sir, please don't be upset with Bertram...It was all my idea for him to get baptized, because that's just our way of making sure that we're all going to Heaven together. I'm sure he didn't mean to trick you, he just wants you to see we don't think bad of anybody. We just want Bertram to be one of us, not just in this life but in the life to come. I know he doesn't want to go against anything you taught him...he's told us how much he loves his family! And I know he is very precious to you. He is special to us, too! I don't know what we'd do without him...he's even lending his voice to our choir, and you'll hear him sing, if you would please just stay for the service..." And, carried away by his zeal for harmony, he reached one paw out to touch the elder buzzard, and the other to touch the younger.

"Get your paws off me and my son!" growled the elder buzzard, and Clancy froze. Then, from deep within Bertram's daddy came a sound, a low, fluid grumbling, and Bertram was horrified, for he knew that his daddy was about to do something nasty. He knew that only complete capitulation to his father's will would stop him from disgracing them both and upsetting his new friends, and he was about to say, "All right, Daddy, let's just go," but the words wouldn't come. What did come was a furiously chittering brown blur from the edge of the gathering right into the midst of the rat and the two buzzards. It was Elwood. He raised himself upon his haunches right in front of Bertram's daddy and vocalized at the top of his lungs. "What's the matter with you?!" scolded the squirrel. "Are you crazy!? This is your *son*! You ought to be ashamed! He's not doing anything wrong! Even if he *was*..." Here the squirrel clenched his little paws into fists. "He's *still* your son! You should be glad he's all right!" And Elwood's tail twitched spasmodically, as if it too was in its own wordless way berating the old buzzard. As for the old buzzard, he regarded the squirrel and gurgled, then turned his scowl upon his wayward son.

"You gonna let them talk to me like that?" he demanded.

Bertram hung his head.

"Don't let him tell you what to do, son," said the squirrel. "He doesn't know how lucky he is. Let him leave if he wants to. It's his loss. We'll look after you, don't worry."

Bertram's daddy began to spread his wings...and his scent...then, slowly, he folded them. "I'm not going nowhere," he said as loftily as his gurgling voice could manage. "My son brought me here, so here I am. And no one's going to look after my son but me." And he glowered down at the squirrel, who took no notice, but leaped away.

"Well!" said Clancy brightly after a moment of uneasy silence, which he decided was as sure a sign as any that the conflict was over. "Should we get started?" Without the slightest lack of aplomb, he turned to Bertram's father. "Sir, you just feel free to take part or just watch, whatever you're comfortable with. Like I said, we welcome everybody just as they are. Now...we'll process in a nice straight line. Ottoline, please lead us in the opening hymn as we go. Friends, we're going to sing a beautiful hymn that Ottoline has adapted for the occasion. It's called *Shall We Gather at the Birdbath*. Here we go!"

And there they went, in a strange procession to be sure, in single file—roughly—some walking, some crawling, some flying low to the ground, repeating, as best they could, line by line, the specially reworded version of an ancient spiritual as Ottoline warbled it out to them. To the occasional automobile that passed the church on the boulevard they were visible only as low small dark shadows in the night, nothing remarkable.

At the birdbath, which was a solid, slightly tilted concrete bowl atop a pitted concrete post, the community formed a loose circle, and their voices trailed off. Clancy leaped up and scrambled to the rim of the birdbath, and regarded with not a little disappointment the mere inch or so of unappealingly dirty water. It was nothing like the nice clear holy water in the baptismal font in the sanctuary, which was unadulterated by fallen leaves and pine needles and dead insects. But this would have to do, and water was water, after all. Hadn't Hertz been baptized in a toilet bowl, for the love of God? It was the blessing, not the water, which counted. Or at least Clancy had reason to believe.

"Praise the Lord!" Clancy cried at the top of his lungs for all to hear. "Welcome, friends. Here we are!"

He looked around at all the figures, large and small, that were focusing their attention upon him. "This is one of the most exciting nights of my life! Tonight, along with some of you, I will claim my name as one of God's children, created in His image and likeness. For those of you who are new to the church, or..." he nodded toward the elder buzzard, "...just visiting, baptism is kind of the official membership badge. It means that your sins, that anything you've done in your life that gets in the way of loving God and your neighbor as yourself, is washed away. Just like any other bath—why, it will make you clean and fresh! But this is a bath for your spirit! It is a fresh start, and so even though you're the same person, you're also something new! You're a Christian! You share something with the church that you never shared before. You belong, and no one can ever take that away from you. Isn't it wonderful?" Clancy raised his forepaws, and, encountering a damp heavy resistance on his shoulders, remembered that Hertz was still draped across him like one of Reverend DeBassompierre's liturgical stoles. Not wanting to make the error of duplicating a baptism, Clancy lifted his friend from off his shoulders and placed him gently on the rim of the birdbath beside him. "Hertz, here, was baptized before the church ever got started, and so he's going to be our sponsor. That's someone who makes sure that we are living up to the promises we make when we got baptized...Okay, Hertz?"

Hertz had no intention of holding any of these creatures to anything, but he knew it would be pointless to argue. He simply coiled himself into a cone on the rim of the birdbath and said nothing.

"So let's get started," said the Reverend Rat. "Now ...I want everyone who has decided to become a Christian tonight to please take a spot up here on the birdbath with me and Hertz. And once we're all up here, I'll come around and baptize each one of you in the name of the Father, and of the Son, and of the Holy Ghost. Ready?"

And with that there was a stir among the gathering. First off, Bertram, with a leap and a brisk flap of his great wingspan, which stirred the air with his cloying odor, landed on the rim of the birdbath to the left of Clancy. Lord, he stinks, Clancy could not help thinking to himself, utterly unconscious that his thoughts echoed the words of Martha to the Lord in the Gospel According to John, but his bearing, he thanked God, did not betray his distaste. We're going to have to work on his hygiene, the rat thought. But not tonight.

Ottoline, closely followed by Steven, her spouse, was the next to rise and alight upon the birdbath rim, right next to Hertz. Then, astonishingly, one of the squirrels, the mother of poor Timmy, in fact, scrambled slowly but steadily up the pedestal and onto the rim of the birdbath. Her husband followed.

"The Lord be with you..." Clancy began, "...and also with me. My friends, this is a night to remember. We're going to welcome five souls...no, six, including mine, into the Kingdom of Heaven. This is where our journey together really begins. We're here to put on Christ, to show the love of the Lord Jesus to every living creature, no matter what. Just look at all of us! We're all different, some of us are birds, some of us are mammals, and some of us are worms...and yet there's one thing that brings us all together, and that's Jesus! Jesus Christ, the son of God, eternally begotten of the Father! And Jesus said, in order to enter into the Kingdom of heaven, and have eternal Life with Him, you have to be born again. And now, I'll just explain a little bit about how this works. Like I said, we are all baptized in the Name of the Father, and of the Son, and of the Holy Ghost, which are the names that God likes to use when he reveals himself to Christians. So when I baptize you, I'm just going to have you step into the birdbath and bow your head so I can reach it, and I'll baptize you by sprinkling your head three times, in the three names of God. That's how we do it in the Episcopal Church. Other churches like to say that you have to go underwater all the way, which would be okay, but we don't have enough water for that. And just so everyone will know what to do, I'll just go first..."

And so saying, Clancy gingerly slipped into the cold, shallow, leaf-strewn water of the birdbath. The chill was unexpected, and he had to grit his teeth against it before he could speak.

"Ooh!" he said. "Just so you know...it's a little nippy! But don't worry...it won't take but a second. Now...the first thing I do is, I ask the candidate...the one being baptized, if he—or she—or they—will renounce Satan and all his works. Satan is a very nasty spirit that tries to trick Christians into doing bad things. So...Clancy?"—Clancy firmly addressed himself—"Do you renounce Satan and all his works?"

"I sure do," replied Clancy the catechumen fervently.

"And do you accept Jesus Christ as your Lord and Savior?"

"Yes!"

"Then I hereby baptize you, Clancy, in the Name of the Father..."

Clancy lowered his head, reached into the water all around him with his cupped paw, and sprinkled a few drops of water on himself.

"And of the Son..." He reapplied the sprinkling.

"And of the Holy Ghost..." He sprinkled a third time. Then he looked around at the congregation.

"Behold! A new creature! Let the church rejoice!" And with that, the rodent, redeemed, stepped back onto the rim of the birdbath and shivered with cold as well as with joy.

A small, rather awkward silence followed, judiciously ended by Ottoline. "That was lovely," she said. "May I go next?"

"Sure," said Clancy happily, and he stepped back into the water, which no longer felt that uncomfortably cold, and he repeated the formula for baptism, first with Ottoline, then Steven. Next the mother squirrel, dour and stoic, stepped into the water, and allowed herself to be redeemed, followed by her husband.

"And now..." said Clancy. "Our newest member, Bertram ...with his father here to support him on his journey...has asked to be baptized...Bertram?"

Bertram cast a swift glance at his daddy, who was standing

apart from the other creatures, before he stepped into the water along with the rat. He bent his long neck until his beak nearly touched the surface of the water, then turned his beak until it was parallel to that surface. Clancy had to stand on tiptoe to sprinkle the sacred drops upon the buzzard's bald temple. "I baptize you, Bertram ...in the Name of the Father, and of the Son, and of the Holy Ghost..."

And with that the great big bird lifted his head, and in so doing seemed to tower above all the others gathered around the water. The moonlight glistened on his damp, featherless head, and his eyes gleamed, lending him a visionary aspect. He did feel differently now than he had the moment before he bowed his head before the rodent. He glanced again at his father, who looked as if he had been frozen in time, his attitude and expression still unyielding. Bertram loved his daddy, and always would, but suddenly somehow he did not feel bound to him in the same way. He was now a part of something the old buzzard would never understand. He didn't really understand it himself.

"Praise the Lord," said Clancy again, breaking into the young buzzard's thoughts, and both creatures stepped out of the cold water. The moon, Bertram noted, was now reflected in the waters of baptism.

"Now, unless anyone else cares to become a baptized Christian tonight..." Clancy paused and looked briefly at the elder buzzard. "I'll just ask the choir to lead us in our recessional hymn...one of my dearest human friend Reverend DeBassompierre's very favorites...*When the Saints Go Marching In*... Please...everyone... feel free to sing along. Ottoline and Steven will sing the first line, and we'll follow right along after them..."

Ottoline and Steven began to croon, and one by one the animals formed a line, with Hertz draped again across Clancy's back, and in that manner they proceeded to the composter for fellowship time.

BERTRAM WAS NOT surprised that his father did not follow, but took off instead in the direction of their nests in the woods. "Oh shoot," said Clancy. "I was looking forward to having a nice talk with him. Well, it is late. I guess he's tired. I'll talk to him real soon, I'm sure..."

Bertram had his doubts.

⚜

AFTER THE FELLOWSHIP time had gone on for a while, Clancy was obliged by nature to slip away into the basement. "Lord," he proclaimed as he defecated in the corner of the basement his Aunt November had long ago designated for that function, "I don't know about you, but I think tonight was a miracle. Six baptisms, Lord, six Christian soldiers now marching in your army of love and joy and peace. I couldn't have done it without you, Lord, and I'm so happy, I don't know what to do. It's almost scary, Lord, to tell you the truth...whoever would have thought that I, Clancy, could actually really make a difference. After all, I'm just a rat, I don't have a whole lot of sense, sometimes I get too excited and I mess everything up, and I'm still a little too stout, which isn't a good example. But I do love you, Lord, and I do believe you've chosen me to spread the Gospel to your own creatures. I just never thought it would happen so fast! You must have big plans for the church, Lord. I just hope I'm what you need..."

⚜

FROM HER PERCH on the power line that connected the church to the transformer on the boulevard, Ottoline had a comprehensive view of the cemetery, the playground, and beyond. Feeling spent from the baptism earlier in the evening as well as the socializing that followed, Steven perched beside her fast asleep. Ottoline, past her laying years, having descended from a long line of strong female characters, found herself in a new phase, and this came as something of a surprise. She rather understood Bertram's standoffish father, unpleasant as he was, for she too had been reared to stick to her own kind. The business of other kinds of creatures was their own. And yet, here she was, officially now, she felt, a member of a species apart, a new community that transcended the old without obliterating past identity. And, she reflected, just in time. Just in time, for she suddenly realized that with her mothering days at their end, she needed to be at the helm of something. She was devoted, of course, to Steven ...but he was, after all, awfully self-possessed. Ottoline was happiest when she was active among others. She required very little sleep, for example, and this wakefulness could be torture when there was nothing to figure out. Since her youngest daughter Lina had left the nest in the spring, Ottoline's own vigilant nature had become a burden to her. But not any longer. Now she again felt suited to her life. Her constitution counted again, as something that others could benefit from. She had qualities lacking in the dear rat, which could supplement his leadership. It was so remarkable how things worked out.

She glanced at Steven, who was still asleep, but who appeared, by the slight occasional twitch of his wings, to be dreaming, and dreaming of flight. Steven was a simple sort, but not without hidden depths that still managed to astonish her. She was surprised, for example, that he had presented himself for baptism. She was glad, certainly, but what did it mean to him? For her it signaled a renewal of her own particularity, with all of its strengths and weaknesses. She'd been only vaguely aware of any need for renewal. Was it the same for him?

She turned her desultory attention to the woods, a not unusual object of her attention. She wasn't looking for anything in particular...she was just watching as the forms of the trees gained substance as the sun rose. Soon it would be morning.

❧ 4 ❧

HOLY MATRIMONY

Clancy could not understand why he seemed to be putting on so much weight. Especially since he had been so busy during the days and weeks following the baptismal ceremony, what with the slight but significant increase in the size of his little parish. While he didn't want to be vain, it was still distressing to be getting so big around. After all, it was possible he might get so thick that he might not be able to squeeze himself out of the basement! It was with this danger in mind that he resolved to exercise not once, but twice a day until he was significantly reduced. And so he was engaged in his exercise regimen, loping up and down the stairs that led up from the basement floor to the door opening onto the main church corridor, when he heard the buzzard call his name.

Clancy stopped mid-climb and looked over to the gnawed-off corner of the crawlspace door. There he saw the clawed toes of one of Bertram's orange feet. "Bertram! Praise the Lord! Hold on just a second!"

"Okay!" gurgled the buzzard agreeably. "Am I bothering you?"

"Not at all!" He was happy to interrupt his exercise. He scrambled down the rest of the stairs, then stopped to catch his breath. "I'll be right out, Bertram. Just a sec..."

Clancy looked around at the dim interior of his cellar, and wished, not for the first or last time, that he had a place in which to consult with his parishioners...an office like Reverend DeBassompierre's, one that wasn't dark and damp and smelly and close like this basement, but was well-furnished, private, inviting, and most importantly, aromatic. He decided to add this to his list of prayers and petitions. In the meantime, he just had to content himself with conducting pastoral business in the open. Most of his parishioners were too big to squeeze through the gap in the crawlspace door anyhow.

Outside, he led the buzzard over into the graveyard for some privacy. "Bertram! I'm glad you came by. Everything all right?"

"Oh yeah," said the buzzard, but his perpetual scowl seemed to convey more moroseness than usual. "Well, Reverend, not everything. This time my daddy's *really* had it with me."

"Why?"

Bertram nodded. "Well...I guess it's my own fault this time. He said that I can't stay in his roost if I'm going to keep going over to the water tower to see Donna. He's real mad at me, Reverend. But I got to go visit Donna, Reverend, she needs me!" And the young buzzard's vocalization grew so gargled as to be nearly incomprehensible.

"Bertram, what in the world?! Who is Donna?!"

For a moment the buzzard's mottled countenance seemed illuminated. "Reverend..." Bertram raised himself to his full height and pulled his wings in close against himself as if to simulate an embrace. "She's my soul mate."

"Your soul mate?'"

"Oh yes, Reverend." Bertram seemed to swell with the magnitude of his feeling. "Oh, she's the most beautiful female in the world. I can't wait for you to meet her, Reverend. I *need* you to meet her. And I want her to meet you too. I've told her about you and the Church and the choir and everything. I told her you'd be nice to her just like you've been nice to me, but she's real...she doesn't really like to be around a whole lot of other creatures. She's had some hard times, Reverend, she had a mate before, and a family, but they put her out, just like my daddy's about to put me out...But she's good, Reverend, she doesn't have any hard feelings. She just misses her young'uns a whole lot, and it makes her feel down..."

Clancy felt uneasy. It dawned on him, in a vague unsettling way, that he'd better be careful. It was like seeing that cat on the edge of the woods.

"So Reverend..." Bertram broke into Clancy's reflections. "Will you talk to my daddy for me?"

"Talk to your daddy!"

Bertram nodded enthusiastically. "Yes, Reverend, please! He ain't gonna listen to me. I've tried to get him to listen, but he won't. He thinks I'm trying to make him look bad. And he thinks I'm witched. He's real mad at me, Reverend. A lot madder than he was about me getting baptized. I don't think I've ever seen him this mad at me." And Bertram shuddered. "But I think he'll listen to you, Reverend. I hope he will. "

"Why would he listen to me? He doesn't like me either! He didn't even stay for fellowship hour after the baptism! I don't think he'll want to hear anything *I* have to say, Bertram."

Bertram hesitated. He knew that his father did not trust anyone outside of the family, and that he didn't like his son associating with creatures outside his species, but he also knew that his father would have found a way to disrupt the baptism even after the squirrel challenged him if he didn't have some respect for and curiosity about the Reverend. His father liked to be in charge, so he couldn't help but feel a grudging admiration for others who were in charge. "He likes your style."

Clancy took this in. His style? That old buzzard liked his style? Well, wasn't that something! He flushed with a pleasure he did not want to feel, for it was doubtlessly based in pride. He shook himself as if to shake off a cobweb.

"But Bertram, what do you even want me to say to your daddy?"

"Tell him that God wants me and Donna to be together."

Clancy's jaw dropped. "Bertram! I can't tell him that! That would be telling a story! I can't say that something is God's will unless God actually tells me I can! I don't even know who this Donna is! Bertram! What in the world!"

"I have to do *something*—I just don't know what!...I don't want my daddy to have to do without me, but Donna needs me, too, Reverend..." said the young buzzard with an almost visible warmth. "She's all alone on that water tower..." And the young buzzard gazed off towards the edge of town. "She's older than I am. She's already laid eggs, you know, she's not like my sisters, she's ...mature. That's another thing my daddy don't like about her. He thinks I can't handle the responsibility of taking care of someone like that. But I know I can, Reverend, 'cause I love her! And besides, the real reason he doesn't like her is because she's a vulture, not a buzzard like us..."

Clancy blinked. He had no idea why a buzzard and a vulture would not make a perfectly suitable match—in fact he did not know that there was any difference between them. The two terms had always seemed to him to apply to the same type of bird, as far as he could tell. But of course, he was not a part of that community, and did not know the intricacies of their identities. What he did know was that Bertram was beside himself in a way that made Clancy more and more uneasy. What in the world, he kept saying to himself.

He decided that he needed more information in order to know what to do next. "Bertram, I hope you don't mind me asking, but what's the difference? Between buzzards and vultures, I mean?"

The commonsense question seemed to calm Bertram a bit. He bent his legs at the knees and settled his bottom on the ground. "I don't know too much about it myself. All I know is what my daddy has always said, you know, that they're just the same as us but they think they're better. We used to all stick together with them, daddy says, but then they decided they didn't want to mix with us and commenced keeping to themselves. They wouldn't scavenge with us and they wouldn't share, and they started calling themselves by that fancy name. We all used to be buzzards back in the old days, daddy says. Daddy says you just can't trust them. And Reverend, he ain't wrong—they always have been snooty to me. But not Donna. She's not like the rest of them, and they don't like her any more either, now that her mate got rid of her. She don't think she's better than us or anybody. And she's so..." And, as if words could only fail him, here the young buzzard raised his beak to the heavens and gurgled.

"I'd love for you meet her, Reverend," he continued when he'd collected himself. "Maybe even before you talk to my daddy."

Clancy was intrigued, to be sure. Bertram was increasingly his friend as well as his parishioner—a situation which Clancy was only dimly beginning to perceive as sticky. He was aware that he would hate for anything to diminish his friend's enthusiasm for the church. And this Donna...well, it seemed as if she just might! Clancy remembered how he'd felt when Hertz went from living in the potted fern above Grace's desk inside the church to living in the composter outside. How happy he'd been for Hertz—that he'd found his purpose in life—and at the same time, how bereft he felt, that his friend would no longer be so free and available to share the daily round. What a blessing it had been, and what a miracle too, that just as Clancy was beginning to wonder if his life was always going to be not much more than eating and sleeping and watching Reverend DeBassompierre and Grace go about the business of running the Church, the Lord called him so unmistakably in that vision, to minister beyond the walls of St. Aloysius. Clancy knew he should have more faith that all would work out for the best, but it wasn't always easy!

"Well, Bertram, if you think it'll help, I'll be happy to meet

Donna," he said. "Tell her she's welcome to come see me any time."

Bertram rose to his feet, then fell to his haunches. "Huzzah! But Reverend, she won't come to see you...no, we'll have to go see her, if that's all right..."

"But how? I can't go all the way out to that water tower!"

"How come?"

"Well, it's so far away! It would take a million years to get there! And we'd have to go through town...Oh no, Bertram, we can't do that! Remember, it's not as easy for me to go places...It's dangerous, and I can't fly like you!"

"Well, sure you can!" said Bertram. "Just hop on!" And he lowered his head and neck to the ground. "I can carry you," he said. "I used to carry my little sisters around all the time before they could fly. And you're just a little thing. Nothing to it. Just hold on tight and I'll get us there before you know it."

The very possibility of taking flight had never before occurred to Clancy, so it was not so much fear he felt at the idea, as it was a kind of visceral rejection. It was as if the buzzard had asked him to turn inside out. "Bertram!" he gasped. "I can't do that! I'd fall and get killed!"

Bertram lifted his head and tilted it quizzically. "Not if you hang on!" he said reasonably enough. "It's real fun, you'll see! It feels good to get away from the ground, and just fly, fly, fly, and soar. You'll enjoy it!" He paused. "Well, you might be a little nervous at first. My sister Zeeney was. But once we get up in the air—and you see everything from up there, the trees just like little sprouts, and the roads and the creeks no wider than your whiskers, and even the big old buildings the people make are just as tiny as rocks—it's real pretty, Reverend, I promise..."

Clancy felt like burying himself underground. Oh, to be so high up that even the buildings lost their massive proportions! What the buzzard was proposing wasn't just frightening, it was against nature! It simply could not be. It was inconceivable that it could lead to anything good whatsoever. Clancy's immediate response expressed an outrage not at his friend who, though caught up in his own desires, was thoroughly devoid of malice, but at the notion itself. "No!" he cried, and the cry was enough to wake the dead beneath their very feet. The sound, shrill and panicked and with a hint of outrage, reached Ottoline, at rest beside her mate on the telephone wire. Instantly she was alert, and motherwit told her that there was something troubling the Reverend. The distress she perceived was not urgent, but it was intense, and the sooner seen to the better. "Steven," she cooed.

"Yup?"

"Darling, it's the Reverend. Did you hear that shriek? Something must be the matter. I want to see what's going on."

"Okay," said Steven, and closed his eyes.

Ottoline took off, following the sound to its source, and came to land on the nearest tombstone. "Reverend...Bertram..." She greeted the two. "What's the matter?! Reverend, you look like you've seen a ghost!"

Clancy was sucking the end of his tail. He didn't answer right away, so the pigeon turned to the buzzard. "Bertram?"

"Well, I was just telling the Reverend, I need him to go talk to my daddy about the vulture I'm in love with, then we decided it would be good if he talked to Donna first, and so I figured I'd fly him out to the water tower where she stays so he could meet her, and..."

Ottoline didn't need to hear any more. "Bertram. Don't be daft."

"But the Reverend can just hang on to me, and..."

"Bertram," Ottoline said again. "You can't just ask the Reverend to do that and expect him to agree. Think for a moment. Put yourself in the Reverend's place. Remember, there was a time before you could trust your own wings. Imagine, being obliged to trust someone else's..."

Bertram was all impatience. "But..."

"Bertram." Ottoline affected sternness. "Be reasonable. I'm sure that this visit you want the Reverend to make isn't so urgent that you can't take the time to properly prepare him to trust you with what is, after all, his life! I'm surprised at you, Bertram. A smart bird like you, and normally so thoughtful—"

Bertram took this in. He felt so good in the sky that it wasn't easy for him to re-experience the uncertainty he'd felt the first time his daddy had ordered him off the perch. But he knew Ottoline was right.

"Reverend," he said. "Miss Ottoline is right. I was just thinking about myself. Do you think maybe we could do a few practice flights, real low to the ground? I promise I won't let you get hurt..."

Clancy's tail end was still in his mouth. Even the notion of flying only two feet above the ground was terrifying. He looked at Ottoline.

Ottoline's composed air seemed to suggest that the buzzard was making a reasonable offer. Clancy didn't want to be difficult. "All right," he said. "But don't go too high! I have a nervous stomach!"

"Huzzah!" croaked and gurgled Bertram. "Thanks, Reverend! Thanks Ottoline!" And he lowered his head and waited for Clancy to mount.

Clancy wasn't happy, but he straddled the buzzard's long neck near its base, wrapped his limbs around it tight, and for good measure wrapped his tail around it as well. The peculiar, over-powering Bertram smell made his eyes smart, but as always it wasn't more than a few moments before he got used to it.

"Ready, Reverend?" asked Bertram, and Clancy couldn't have answered to save his life. He was petrified. Ottoline, neither unaware, nor unconcerned, nor unamused, chimed in for him. "He's ready, Bertram. Holding on tight as a tick. Now, Bertram, listen to me. Go *no higher* than the top of the gate. And don't go far. Just to the edge of the graveyard and back. And if the Reverend tells you to land, land. Do you understand me?"

"Yes ma'am," said Bertram. Then he stood and stretched out his wings, and Clancy felt his stomach drop. He squeezed his eyes shut. One tremendous, and to Clancy very loud and sickening flap and the two creatures were airborne. Clancy did not dare to look, but he could sense that he was quite a bit higher than the top of the gate, but by no means as high as birds as large as Bertram normally flew. He could feel himself going forward at a faster speed than he had ever moved before, and the rhythmic pulse of the buzzard's musculature underneath Clancy's body was unsettling. He was completely dependent upon another creature, and he did not care for it one bit. But within the terror, he had to admit, was a thread of exhilaration.

A midair hairpin U-turn caused him to gasp and shriek and tighten his full-bodied grip around the buzzard's tough neck. After three or four more great flaps of those wings, there was a gentle descent, and then they were on the ground again. Clancy continued to cling to the buzzard's neck like a barnacle, until Ottoline approached, and addressed him directly. "Reverend," she said. "That was actually a very typical short flight, although the U-turn *was* rather extreme. How do you feel? Would you like to take a longer, higher flight now? Or wait?"

"Wait," said Clancy, not yet ready to let go.

⚜

OVER THE NEXT few days they practiced flying, taking incrementally longer and higher trips, and while Clancy never became comfortable, and in fact, in a certain sense became less so, he did manage to become confident that he had it in his power not to lose his grip on the one thing keeping him aloft and alive. Bertram was, of course, intensely eager for the practice sessions to end, so that he could take his pastor to meet his beloved.

One evening, after they had flown over the edge of the forest at a height of about two hundred feet, Clancy decided he was ready to get the whole ordeal over with. "All right," he announced, while still clinging for dear life to Bertram even after their safe landing. "I think I'm about as ready as I'll ever be. Should we go tomorrow?"

"Sure!" Bertram was of course overjoyed. "Huzzah! You'll love her, Reverend, as much as I do, I promise! I'll be here at the composter at sundown, and we'll head on over to the water tower. Oh Reverend, you're the best!"

Clancy felt obscurely irritated. He figured that this business of flying was affecting his level of patience.

He went home to his cellar and steeled his will against the temptation to raid the pantry to settle his nervous stomach. He brought together his front paws, and began to address the Almighty. "Lord!" he prayed. "Please help me tomorrow. I'm scared of taking such a long flight, even though I know Bertram won't let anything bad happen if he can help it. And I'm also nervous about meeting this Donna. I'm sure she's nice, but Bertram is just too..." He ground his teeth as he tried to articulate his vague sense that something was amiss. "...too happy. What should I do, Lord? Lord, I just pray that you'll guide me...and Bertram too. And Lord, I just want You to know that I do trust in You, even though it might not look like it, when I'm up there scared to death. In Your Precious Name, Lord, Amen."

❧

THEY TOOK off early in the evening, while a bit of daylight remained. This was not Clancy's preference; he did not relish the prospect of flying home in the dark of night, but he knew it was for the best. Ottoline, of course, was there to see them off. "You are going to be just fine, Reverend," she assured him. "Bertram is a very competent aviator. And you have a strong and determined grip. If you start to feel dizzy or uneasy, just take deep breaths. And remember, there is no place that God is not."

It was good and necessary advice. Because the flight to the water tower was higher and faster and more extraordinarily terrifying than Clancy could have imagined. As the two of them gained altitude, and the church and the boulevard and the forest dwindled in size beneath them, Clancy felt as if some invisible thread tethering him to all that was dependable was nearly stretched to the breaking point. He tightened his full body grip around the base of Bertram's neck, all the while worried that he might be throttling or causing pain to his pilot and friend, but Bertram didn't seem to mind. Over the boulevard and into the city they soared, in a mostly straight line so as to cause as little distress to the rat as possible, until finally, as they approached the tower, they began to make a swift and steady descent. "Here we are!" called Bertram over the rush of the wind. "Hang on, Reverend!...I gotta flap hard to slow us down, so you might experience some turbulence, but it's a real smooth landing; there's a platform underneath the tank, and that's where she lives. Here we go..."

Clancy's grip, already tight, became viselike, as the base of the buzzard's wings flexed beneath him and the landing was, indeed, smooth, though still terrifying. They came to perch on the railing that ran around a metal platform just beneath the base of the massive water tower. And there on that platform was a creature very much like Bertram in form, though broader. It moved, and in so doing stirred the still air beneath the massive, slightly convex underside of the municipal water tower. The smell of her was much like Bertram's odor, although somewhat brinier. "Donna!" gurgled Bertram, and those two syllables managed to convey pure adoration. "This is Reverend Clancy, the pastor of my church. Reverend, this is Donna, my...my sweetie."

Clancy stared as the female vulture stepped forward. She was an astonishing sight. Like Bertram, she had feathers of a variegated darkness, a long bare neck, a formidably tough-looking pointed and hooked beak, a glowering brow and a mottled, rather crusty reddish complexion. But there was something in her bearing that lent all these unfortunate features, so common to her species, a truly grotesque and regal magnificence. She spoke, and her vocalizations had the same coarse gurgling quality as Bertram's, but with a resonance that brought to Clancy's mind the lowest notes achievable by the Hammond Organ played at every Sunday morning service in St. Aloysius Sr.

She spoke directly to Clancy. "Hello, Reverend. Bertram's told me so much about you. I'm happy to meet you. But I wasn't expecting visitors this evening. I apologize if I'm...taken off guard. It's been a long day."

"That's all right," said Clancy. But he realized as he spoke that he had already forgotten her name! He searched his little mind, but could only retrieve such generic and formal terms of address as 'ma'am,' 'lady,' and even 'Your Eminence,' all terms that were drawn from Reverend DeBassompierre's discourse. These terms seemed to fit his sense that he was in the presence of someone remarkable.

She stepped over to stand close to Bertram. "I don't know how much Bertram has told you about me, Reverend, but..."

"Oh, Bertram's just told me that you're ...very nice."

The female vulture lowered her gaze, then lifted it to look directly at Clancy.

"Bertram is very nice himself. Too nice for his own good, I'm afraid. He probably hasn't told you that I'm an outcast. And I have to be very careful, or I could be harmed, if not killed, by my own kin. It's a long, complicated story, but you should know that they have taken my own fledglings from me.... I'm considered unfit to raise them. They'll be encouraged to forget me, and if not, to despise me. I brought shame to the group. At least that's what most of my family thinks. Because I struck up an acquaintance with dear Bertram here, when we happened to mutually but independently find a particularly choice carcass and decided to share it. To make a long story short, this ended up with me being accused of infidelity, of disgracing the group. Bertram's family, I think, is not as harsh, though I understand that they're also suspicious. At any rate, I've brought shame. But, Reverend, I can't bring myself to agree with my mate and the others that we're somehow superior to Bertram's group, and that we must never, ever share. It's nonsense, Reverend. They have my fledglings, and I could be taken back in, I think, if I just admitted I was wrong and the rest of them are right. But by now my younger ones probably don't even remember me. And the older ones...well, their father is angry with me, and bitter, and my being there could make things...tense, and perhaps even dangerous for them as well as for myself in the long run. What should I do, Reverend? Bertram tells me that you are very wise, and that you've found the answer to everything..."

For the first time in a long time, Clancy thought of his own mother, from whose neglect Aunt November had saved him. Had she missed him the way this mother missed her babies? He moved forward, as if away from the thought.

"Ma'am, all I know is that Jesus loves you and loves your children, too. Do you know about Jesus? Has Bertram had a chance to share the Gospel with you? Jesus loves you, and loves your children, and loves your enemies too. Jesus says that we must pray for those who persecute us."

"What does this mean, to pray?"

Clancy said the first thing that came to his mind. "Well, it means to ask for what you want."

"Well, I want to know that my children are loved. And I want to be able to see them and to let them know that I love them." The majestic creature's dark eyes seemed to glisten for a moment.

"Well then, God will answer your prayers," said Clancy with bright, ready certainty. "All you have to do is ask, and put your trust in Him, and He will give you all that you need...as long as you pray in the Spirit. Just say, Jesus, I'm lost, and I need help, and I don't know what to do. Please give me a sign. And He will! You just have to be patient."

The vulture named Donna tilted her head and regarded Clancy with what seemed like wonder for a long moment, then turned to Bertram. "Dear One," she said. "You are right. It's all very mysterious. This Jesus must be a convincing person, if you think He can make our families see things differently. But if you really think He can help..."

"Oh, He'll help, Donna, if the Reverend says He will. He's real real good at figuring things out," Bertram said fervently. "I don't understand it much myself, but the Reverend here does. He talks to Jesus all the time, and Jesus always tells him just what to do."

Clancy started. While the buzzard had the right idea, it was certainly not that simple. But before he could get his thoughts together sufficiently to speak, Donna spoke up.

"Where can I find Jesus?" mused Donna. "I'd like to meet Him."

"In our church," said Clancy without hesitation. "You can meet Him this Sunday, if you would like to join us."

⚜

THE FLIGHT HOME TO ST. Aloysius was not the same as the flight to the water tower, for it was cloudless and dark, the moon was nearly full, and a spray of stars was scattered above. It was very beautiful, and fascinating too, to observe the lights of the little coastal city from so high above. But it was still too scary for Clancy to keep his eyes open for very long. For the most part he kept them shut tight, clinging to the buzzard with all his strength and gritting his teeth as well.

Finally they landed in the center of the graveyard. Clancy dismounted and skittered in circles around Bertram, for the solid warm gravelly ground beneath his paws felt so good. When he finally stopped, Bertram settled himself on his rear so as to come as close as he could to eye level with his pastor.

"Isn't she special, Reverend?"

Clancy was still euphoric after having landed safe and was more than willing to agree. "She's real cute, Bertram. I enjoyed meeting her, and I look forward to seeing her at church this Sunday and getting to know her better."

"I love her so much, Reverend..." Bertram said.

Clancy had the distinct feeling that the buzzard was not so much speaking to communicate as he was speaking to relieve himself of the pressure of an ever-intensifying emotion. With this realization Clancy found himself struck, as if by lightning, with a jarring sense of the irrational, unfathomable power of what he dimly recognized as romantic love. His ears pricked, and the tufts of fur that crowned them stood straight on end as if electrified. He realized that yet again, though in a different sense than when he was airborne, he was out of his element. Oh Lord, he thought to himself, what am I supposed to say?

"Bertram," he said, not at all sure he would even be heard. "Can we set a time tomorrow to get together and talk? I hate to say it, but I think all the flying has upset my stomach. I think I better go in and rest..."

"Okay," the buzzard agreed cheerfully, not in the least perturbed or concerned. He stood slowly and stretched himself, like a sleeper awakening. "See you tomorrow."

"God bless you, Bertram," Clancy said severely. Then, while the buzzard was still there to hopefully scare away any predators, the rat scampered quickly to the shelter of the church building.

⚜

THE NEXT MORNING Ottoline kept an eye out for any sign of Clancy, as she was curious as to how his first real flight and his visit with Bertram's female friend had gone. Somewhat later than usual, he emerged from the cellar and trotted over to the compost heap as was his usual habit, to say good morning to Hertz. Ottoline fluttered down from her wire and joined him.

"Not to be nosy, Reverend, but I *am* curious. How was your 'maiden flight?'

Now that the ordeal was past, Clancy was able to look back

on it with more calm, especially after a decent night's sleep and a light breakfast of Grace's apple peelings. "Not too bad," he allowed. "Once I got used to all that noise.... the flapping, the wind in my ears...and, you know, I never knew it was so cold up there, I don't know how you all don't get sick! Anyway, it's over with now, thank the Lord. I'm just so glad you made sure we practiced first. That Donna does live a long way off...and way up on that water tower!"

Ottoline was pleased. "And Donna...tell me about her. What is she like? Is she a good match for our Bertram?"

Clancy had hoped no one would ask him about that. He wasn't at all sure what he thought, or even if it was right for him to share his thoughts about one parishioner's business with another parishioner. But he figured that Ottoline was in a sense his right paw, and more than just another member of the church. And maybe her female perspective was exactly what he needed.

"Well..." he began. "She's very nice."

This, of course, communicated nothing, but Ottoline was patient and silent. "Well," Clancy began again, "She's real...interesting. She seems real smart, kind of like Reverend DeBassompierre, so smart that maybe it makes some others feel like she's trying to be better than them. Yes, I think that's what the problem is. It's like a while back, when Reverend DeBassompierre was having trouble with the Vestry. He wanted to start up a whole lot of Sunday school classes about some people called the Cappadocians, but the vestry said no one would be interested, because no one but a priest would know who they were. Anyway, Donna's own folks won't let her even see her own young ones, and they think she shouldn't be nice to Bertram. So she doesn't have anyone but Bertram to talk to, and she's so smart and really kind of exciting to be around, and I can see why Bertram likes her so much, but..."

Ottoline waited.

Clancy looked around as if he were worried that Bertram might be nearby and listening. "Well, I just think Bertram isn't really thinking about what's best for everyone...I don't know...I don't think I should tell him this, but I sort of understand why his daddy doesn't want him to get involved with her. I mean, his daddy shouldn't be so mean about it, but there's something about her that's just..." Clancy reached for his tail. "I don't know. There's just something about her. I can't put my paw on it."

"Do you think she loves him?" Asked Ottoline.

Clancy dropped his tail. That was it, exactly. It didn't take a lot of experience as a counselor to recognize that Bertram and the fascinating Donna did not feel quite the same way about one another. "I...I'm not sure. I think she cares about him, but...well, he's just so...it's like she's all he wants to think or talk about. And she...well, I think she has a lot more to think about than Bertram..."

"Poor Bertram," said Ottoline. "He's going to need our support. This isn't going to be easy for him, no matter what happens. He's head over heels."

Clancy looked at the pigeon questioningly.

"Love is sorrow as much as joy," said Ottoline. "But of course you know that, Reverend..."

Clancy blinked. Did he? For a moment he felt unsure of just about everything.

Ottoline looked at him with not a little affection. Compared to her, he was in many ways very naïve. And yet, he was the leader of the church; he possessed a kind of authority that the naiveté only enriched.

"I've always held," she said, "that love is so powerful that it can assume just about any form in which it is possible to appear. It can bring things together and tear them apart. It can join you to another soul or to your own special destiny. I think it is never without danger, at least not for long."

Clancy felt torn. On the one paw, he didn't think that love should mean trouble. Love was supposed to be like God, perfect and almighty! On the other paw, he sensed that Ottoline was, as usual, right.

"I'm just worried..." he said, picking his way into his impressions as if crawling in the dark. "It's like...he doesn't really care about anything except her, or unless it has something to do with her. And I don't think she wants him to feel that way, but she can't stop it any more than I can...it seems so..."

"Crazy," supplied Ottoline.

"Well, I didn't want to say that, but I don't know what else to say. It's crazy, isn't it, to ...to ..."

"Be in love...?" Ottoline would have smiled if she could.

"I guess I just don't understand," he said.

Ottoline chuckled. "It's puzzling sometimes. But it does feel wonderful to fall in love, and no matter what happens, I think Bertram will grow from the experience; we all do in the long flight..."

Clancy regarded Ottoline wonderingly. Here she was, the epitome of mature reason and warm serenity, and yet she seemed to understand, if not relate to, Bertram's craziness. Clancy felt rude asking, but it couldn't be avoided. "But you and Steven aren't crazy!" he said.

"No?" said Ottoline, unable to suppress more chuckling. "I suppose not. After all this time. But in the beginning..." Neither Ottoline nor Clancy realized consciously that she was echoing the first words of Scripture, the account of Creation. "In the beginning, we were very reckless. Completely absorbed. It really was as if nothing and no one else mattered..."

"You and Steven?!" cried Clancy.

Ottoline looked at the reverend. Oh, he had a lot to learn! "Yes, Steven and I indeed...if these trees could talk!" she said. "When we first met...well, it was all so new. Starting something new, don't you think, is always a little crazy, isn't it? A new church, a new relationship...anything new has to be disturbing...Then, you do your best to make it fit into your life as it stands... Bertram, I think, might be too young, and his support from his family is too rigid and conditional, he doesn't really have the resources to control his feelings right now. But I think we can help him. The church, I mean. Isn't that part of our mission?"

Clancy began to feel like himself again. Of course. Of course. Ottoline, Lord love her, as Aunt November would have said, was absolutely right. Bertram might be making a big mistake, but it was Clancy's duty as his pastor to help him rather than to judge him. "You're so right, Ottoline!" Clancy said, and his characteristic ebullience was once more a feature of his vocalizations, raising their pitch considerably. "Bertram just needs to know that we're here for him."

"And that we love him," added Ottoline, "with the sort of love that can bear with stormy feelings."

Clancy wasn't sure precisely what Ottoline meant by that, but it sounded good, so he agreed. The two creatures were silent, but companionably so, for the remainder of their morning stroll, which ended where it began, at the composter.

"There's Steven," she said, looking up at her mate standing on top of the ornamental belfry. "See you later, Reverend dear."

"See you later, Ottoline," said Clancy. She fluttered up and away, and Clancy stood in the familiar stench and shade of the composter, glad to be near its teeming life, yet alone with his own teeming thoughts. Lord! Leading a congregation was getting more and more complicated with every single day! And his was just a baby congregation, really no more than seven or eight regular creatures who could be considered members. He couldn't imagine what it would be like to have to care for a church even as big as struggling St. Aloysius Sr.! Again he gave thanks and praise to the Lord for Ottoline and her good sense.

He gazed out past the composter to the churchyard and the forest beyond. Lord, he loved the world and his exciting new place within it, but there was just so much he did not comprehend. So how then could he have imagined that he could lead? He supposed it was just one of those mysterious ways in which the Lord was said to work. He looked up at the sky and happened to see a group of unidentifiable birds flying in forma-

tion, from east to southwest. He received it as a sign—that
indeed, all God's creatures need one another. His thoughts
returned, as if to a wound itching as it healed, to the matter of
Bertram and his wild passion for Donna, and likewise to Ottoline's tame love for Steven. There was something so unsettling
about it all that he found himself thinking too of that feral cat
that he'd seen crouching and staring from the edge of the forest,
twitching its tail irregularly and ominously. This crazy thing that
—like God's love and the good Christian love of the church and
of good Christians like Aunt November—was referred to as love,
that seemed so different and so much more dangerous than the
gentle affection he felt for himself and for almost everything he
could think of, made him want to run and hide, to cover himself
so thoroughly with some obscuring material that he would be
hidden from sight. And yet, he recognized that the crazy love
was just as necessary as his gentle love, and the all-encompassing
love of God and Jesus, and the power that They gave, to render
life more than mere living. Without the wild love, there was only
mating. With that sudden realization, Clancy felt his entire body
shiver and flush with warmth. And that brought him to the difficult truth that there was more to his own self than he wanted to
know about. "Oh Lord." He closed his eyes and prayed. "Help."

❦

THAT EVENING BERTRAM, having waited for what felt to him
like an endless day to discuss his beloved with the Reverend,
tapped on the crawlspace door with his beak and called for
Clancy. "Reverend? Are you busy?"

Clancy wasn't busy—in fact, he'd been napping. To his
chagrin, he'd been unable to resist the remains of a sweet roll
he'd come across in Grace's wastebasket, and the simple carbo-
hydrates had knocked him out. "Just a minute!" he called. "I'm
coming!"

But it took a few minutes for him to shake off drowsiness

and wash his face with the condensation dripping from the water heater. By the time he crawled out of the cellar and over to where Bertram waited by the composter, most of the stars were out.

Bertram was trying to be patient, but the moment he saw Clancy he rushed over. "Reverend! I was just over at the water tower talking to Donna! She really, really liked you, Reverend! I knew she would. She said that I should trust you, that she could tell you care about me a whole lot, and I told her that I know, that you're my best friend on top of being my Reverend! I'm glad the two of you like each other! That means my daddy's wrong about both of you! I sure wish he wasn't so hardheaded. I wonder if he'll ever change..."

Clancy didn't think so, but he held his tongue.

Bertram didn't linger for long on that painful subject. "Anyway, Reverend, Donna said that she's gonna try to make it to church this Sunday, because she really does want to meet Jesus. She says she hopes he's here. I told her that I haven't seen him, but that if you said he would be here, that he would be."

Clancy reached for his tail. Oh Lord, he thought. Here we go again.

"Oh Bertram," he said. "I thought you understood. Jesus is always with us. We just don't see Him the same way we see each other. We see him in our hearts. You tell Donna she's welcome in Church any time, like I said, but she doesn't have to be here to pray to the Lord. She can pray right there on the water tower. You don't have to come to church to talk to Jesus, but it does help, because He likes to be where Christians gather together in his name."

"Oh," said Bertram, and to Clancy he sounded a little put out.

"What's wrong, Bertram?"

The young buzzard looked at the ground. "Oh...I just wanted her to come with me this Sunday, so that she can meet everybody, but if she can talk to Jesus without coming to church, she probably won't come. She's real shy, Reverend, and she doesn't feel safe around a crowd, I guess on account of how her own have treated her. I was just hoping I could help her feel like she was one of us..."

Clancy thought of Donna, and in picturing her in his mind's eye, so compelling yet aloof and conspicuous in her extraordinary appearance, it was easy to imagine that she would feel uncomfortable at a Sunday morning service.

Bertram looked up now at the richly sparkling night sky. "I just wish there was some way to show her that I'll always love her and protect her and I won't let anything happen to her and that my friends will love her too..."

Before the words were out of his mouth, Clancy wondered what had gotten into him. "Well, we could have a wedding..."

❦

OF COURSE, it was necessary to explain to Bertram what it meant, to have a wedding, and to be married in the church, in the sight of God. "It's kind of like baptism," Clancy said. "Except there's no water. We just have the two of you stand with me in front of the whole congregation, and the two of you repeat your vows, and I seal the marriage, which means that God has joined you together."

Bertram was overjoyed. He wanted nothing more than to be joined together with Donna. "I can't wait!" he said. "It sounds fantastic! What are vows?"

"Vows are..." Clancy considered. "Well, I guess it's another word for promises. You make promises to each other and to the church...and to the Lord, of course...that you'll love each other and help each other and stay together through good times and bad times, and that you won't..." Clancy paused here, not sure how to approach the matter of marital fidelity, about which his own understanding was sketchy. He wished Ottoline were there. "...you won't love anyone as much as you love each other."

"I promise!" crowed Bertram, as if the actual ceremony was underway.

Clancy couldn't help but be uplifted by his friend's enthusiasm. He began to trust that the Spirit had led them to precisely where they ought to be...the altar. Still, it was his duty to be sure that the buzzard appreciated the gravity of the matter. "Well, don't make any promises yet! You haven't even asked Donna if she wants to get married. She has to want it too, you know."

"Oh, she does!" Bertram said. "She loves me! She says she doesn't know what she'd do without me. But I'll ask her! I'll go ask her right now!"

And with that Bertram was off, leaving a whiff of his scent and a bemused Clancy in the shadow of the composter. Lord, said Clancy to himself, I hope he's right.

৩৯৩

CLANCY WAS GLAD WHEN, not too much later, Ottoline descended from the ornamental belfry. "Oh Lord, Ottoline!" he said. "Now Bertram wants to marry Donna! It looks like we're going to have a wedding!"

"Wedding?"

Clancy explained again, with an emphasis on the ceremonial aspect.

"Well, that sounds lovely," said Ottoline. "And a perfect opportunity to introduce Donna to the community. But I understand your concern. It sounds like a very decisive step. I'm not sure Bertram is ready and it sounds like it might be a step too far for Donna..." She settled herself on the ground thoughtfully. "But on the other wing, it may prove to be catalytic. In any event, it should be a festive occasion..."

Clancy was eager to agree. "I guess it won't hurt Bertram to ask! Will it?"

Ottoline decided not to answer that.

"Reverend!" Bertram was once again at the crawlspace door at dusk. "Reverend! Are you in there? She said yes! She said yes, Reverend, she wants to marry me!"

Clancy had just come down into the basement after spending the afternoon, as usual, observing Reverend DeBassompierre, who had been unhappily answering telephone calls and emails, Grace having taken the afternoon off for a colonoscopy prep. It had been interesting watching his mentor struggle with the logistics of such matters as scheduling vestry meetings and ordering flowers, and Clancy was heartened to discover that even highly experienced pastors are subject to complete bewilderment. Feeling thus encouraged, he was not disinclined to share in Bertram's jubilation. He squeezed himself outside and into Bertram's shadow.

"She said yes!" crowed the buzzard.

"Yes, I heard!" said Clancy. "That's wonderful, Bertram."

"She's going to marry me!" Bertram proclaimed.

Here Clancy felt a tug of apprehension in his bowels, for even though he was within inches of his friend, Bertram continued to vocalize as if he were still in the cellar. It's like he doesn't even realize I'm here! thought Clancy.

For a few moments, the two creatures stood in front of the composter, together but absorbed within their own thoughts. Finally Clancy's presence registered upon Bertram, and he crowed again, still rapturously, but not so loud. "She said yes, Reverend!"

"Congratulations. I'm so happy for you, Bertram!" Clancy said, and this response seemed to stick. He took a deep breath. "I guess this means we should start planning the ceremony. Of course, we'll want to make sure we have plenty of time to make arrangements and let everybody know..."

At this Bertram blinked. "Oh! Wow! I guess you're right. I guess I was hoping we could get married tomorrow."

"Oh, I don't think that's enough time. This is a very special event, you know, Bertram, and I'm sure you want it to be just right. Now, here are some things we need to think about...do you want to have the choir sing anything in particular? Do you want a reception after the ceremony? And Bertram...are you going to ask your folks to come...?"

Looking back, Clancy felt that all the trouble began with that last suggestion, but at the time it just seemed natural. It did have an immediate effect upon the atmosphere. Bertram's bright euphoria dimmed like the sun going behind a cloud. His head bowed low. "Oh yeah..." he gurgled, markedly subdued. "I did think about that...but Reverend, I don't think they'll come. I'm not sure I should even tell them about it. My daddy gets so mad when it comes to Donna..." He shuddered involuntarily. "Do I have to ask them, Reverend?"

"You don't have to..." Clancy said. "After all, it's your wedding...and Donna's too, of course. But Bertram, don't you think they deserve a chance to share your special day? After all, they are your family, for better or for worse..." Clancy knew he'd heard that last phrase somewhere before, but he couldn't think where.

"I guess you're right, Reverend," Bertram said. "You always are." He perked up. "I know! *You* can ask daddy! With all this about the wedding, I'd forgot! You and daddy were going to have another talk! You want me to go get him now?"

Clancy had also forgotten, and wasn't particularly glad to be reminded. that this whole scenario had begun with Bertram asking him to mediate. Clancy dreaded the prospect of another difficult conversation with Bertram's intimidating daddy, but he knew that he didn't really have a good reason to refuse. Hadn't he just said that the old buzzard deserved a chance? And after all, wasn't this his duty, in a sense, to intercede? Oh Lord, he said to himself. When all this is over with, I need to take a vacation.

What a vacation would mean for him, who was anxious whenever he was away from the familiar, he did not know. But

Reverend DeBassompierre had said the exact same thing aloud to himself at one point that afternoon between phone calls, and it just sounded apropos to Clancy in his current state of mind.

"Okay." Clancy reached for his tail, and Bertram was off into the treetops like a rocket.

🐀

CLANCY COULDN'T HELP but hope that the old buzzard would not be any more eager to meet again than he himself was, but it wasn't long before father and son emerged from the woods and descended into the churchyard.

"I'm gonna leave ya'll alone to talk," said Bertram with a rapidity that suggested real nervousness. "I'll be back in a little bit, all right, Daddy? You just let the Reverend explain everything. I'll see ya'll..." And he took off into the trees, before either Clancy or his father could respond, leaving the rat and the old buzzard to regard one another. The elder buzzard stood above him like a brick wall, unscalable and impenetrable, and his black eyes, ringed in red and yellow crepey skin, were hard.

"Thanks for stopping by," said Clancy, meek and determined. "Bertram wants me to let you know I'm going to perform a special ceremony for him. He has asked me to join him and his friend Donna in Holy Matrimony. That means that they are going to be a part of each other's lives forever, and that they are bound together in the eyes of God and of our church. Bertram has shared with me that your family and Donna's family don't get along too well, but I'm sure that's something you can work on."

The old buzzard did not move a muscle nor utter a sound, yet still managed to convey absolute denial. Clancy felt as if he was wading into cold mud.

"Sir, I know you really love your son, and you worry about him making good decisions..." Said Clancy, with a note of hopelessness that surprised even himself. "But you should realize that no matter what happens he's going to be just fine in the end because all of us here at St. Aloysius Jr. are going to support him. So please don't worry. We are going to be here for him and look after him and support him and even try to warn him if we think he might be doing something that isn't good for him. That's what churches do for their members! I want you to know, if I thought Bertram was making a mistake, I wouldn't encourage him. But I've met Donna, and I think she's real nice. I can see why you might think she's...strange. But really, she's just as sweet as she can be..."

The elder buzzard remained impassive, forbidding, malodorous, above all silent and haughty. Clancy, with something of his Aunt November's sense of social decorum, could not experience this manner as anything but ill. Rude. He felt his indignation rise.

"Sir, I wish you would at least answer me."

The old buzzard, though remaining immobile, seemed somehow to advance. "She's tainted," he hissed. "Even her own won't have her with them. And you want my son to..."

"Sir, it isn't what I want, it's what Bertram wants. And sir, I may not know much, but I know you have to follow your heart. And Bertram just loves Donna to pieces, and there's nothing wrong with that. She is very sweet. It's not her fault that her family is so ugly to her." Clancy knew before the next words were out of his snout that he was going to make Bertram's daddy even more angry. That was the last thing he wanted to do. But it was as if the words had a will of their own...it was not unlike the experience he had sometimes when preaching, of something or someone speaking through him, in spite of his own ignorance. And these words came, leaping like jackrabbits over his timid qualms. "And the way you are acting to Bertram is no different."

This time the old buzzard did advance. Clancy held his ground, but he was sore afraid. "Well, it isn't," he said, not quite as boldly as he had when it seemed as if the Spirit Itself was speaking through him. "Don't you see? You're making your own son choose between you and his own true feelings. Now why would you want to do that? That's an awful thing to do to someone you're supposed to love."

The old buzzard stretched his neck high and looked down upon the rat. "Seems to me you don't know nothing about raising up a son. But you want to tell me how to raise mine."

Clancy, now thoroughly in the shadow of the larger creature, felt as never before his very real lack of life experience. For a dark moment he felt permeated by the dense justice of the old buzzard's observation. What *did* he know about being a parent? Nothing. And something told him he never would. Mindless and miserable, he reached for his tail, lifted it to his mouth, and began to gnaw.

"Stop that!" hissed a voice, but it was not the voice of the old buzzard. It came from the composter. Clancy looked over and saw his friend's familiar tip protruding from the aerator slot. But just for a split second, for Hertz withdrew, having said what he came to say. It was enough. Clancy was not alone. He took courage.

"I may not know about that," he said. "But I'm a pastor, and I have friends, and I have Jesus, and that's enough for me. Now, sir, you are welcome to join us anytime you like, and you know that we would love for you to attend the wedding with your family, but if you're going to be ugly to Donna..."

"There ain't going to be no wedding," said the old Buzzard, "nor nothing like it. Bertram ain't coming back here neither." And the old buzzard spread his tailfeathers, as if to claim more space.

"I think that should be up to Bertram," said Clancy. Then, for good measure, "and God."

The old buzzard then emitted a long, somehow aggressive and highly odiferous hiss. It seemed to signify a threat of some sort, though Clancy could not be sure. The offensiveness of the odor was in fact so intense that the rat instinctively moved a few steps back. He wished he hadn't, for he didn't want to look like he was intimidated, even though he certainly was. But he was also not a little angry, and this assault upon his most delicate of senses made him even angrier. Any thought of Christian charity was absent from his spirit at the moment.

"If you are going to be nasty like that, you will have to leave this church," he said. "It may not look like much to you, but this is holy ground."

Bertram's daddy hissed again. The noxious odor made Clancy's eyes sting. He blinked, and this made him feel obscurely that he was letting his dear friend Bertram down. "Stop that!" he screeched, echoing Hertz's words, and to some degree Hertz's indomitable spirit. "Go away and don't come back here until you can show some respect!" And with that Clancy did something he'd never done before. He bared his teeth at another creature.

The old buzzard figuratively and somewhat literally exploded —he hissed, he spat, he seemed to spew in every direction from every orifice on his body some putrescent fluid or substance as he spread his wings, lifted his clawed feet and rose into the air directly above Clancy, so that for a moment the rat was again completely overshadowed. But it was only the buzzard's shadow that made any contact with him. It was as if, even in his rage, the old buzzard was taking care to not actually inflict damage. It was purely a display, this outburst. Clancy was alarmed, but not terrified. He crouched close to the ground, but watched as the angry bird rose higher and higher in ever expanding circles above before darting off into the treetops.

⚭

AFTER A FEW MINUTES Bertram emerged from the woods, not by wing, but walking in his ungainly, mincing way as if to signal his dejection. "Daddy wouldn't listen, would he? I ain't surprised." The young buzzard shook his bald head with knowing sadness.

Clancy too could only shake his head.

"That's all right." Bertram settled heavily on the ground

beside Clancy. "I didn't really think he'd change his mind. Not about Donna."

Clancy didn't know what to say. What was there to say, when it seemed as if he'd made things worse than before? "I'm sure he'll calm down," he said, but not with much conviction. "Your daddy loves you," he added, and here he felt he was on firmer ground. But not as firm as it should be. There was, he thought, some love in the old buzzard's adamant demand for obedience, but it was not the sort of love that Clancy would recommend. He remembered—without wanting to—his own Aunt November's cold disapproval when she'd discovered that he, Clancy—her Precious Angel, as she always called him—was spending his afternoons hiding behind the bookcase in the office of the newly hired and, to her, suspiciously young and studious Reverend DeBassompierre. "I don't like his attitude," she said of her beloved Reverend Bickel's replacement, and she offered no reason why. "Don't pay any attention to him, Precious Angel. He's not nice." It was the first time that Clancy could ever remember feeling that his Aunt was not being fair. He thought the new rector was, in a manner of speaking, more exciting than old Reverend Bickel, who had died suddenly on the golf course. Young, tall, dark-haired and dark-eyed Reverend DeBassompierre was such a striking presence at the altar, and he knew so much about the Bible, and all the old languages it was written in, and his sermons, though long and hard to follow, still somehow communicated a brilliance that Clancy found fascinating. But Aunt November missed Reverend Bickel terribly and thought it was all hogwash. "I believe we may have to find us another church home, Precious Angel," Aunt November said with steely seriousness not two days before she died. Which of course left Clancy feeling an uncomfortable relief alongside his sincere grief.

Bertram sat beside him, looking as downtrodden as only a buzzard can look, like a solitary figure on a barren limb. "I feel so dadgum bad," he said. "I don't know what to do."

"It'll be all right," Clancy said, as much to himself as to Bertram. "You just try not to worry." Then inspiration struck. "And you can always pray. Pray for your daddy. He must be hurting too. Even if he doesn't know it. Clancy stood for a moment on his hind paws, exactly as if he were on top of the composter, preaching away.

"And Bertram, please try to be patient. Remember, just because you've become a Christian, it doesn't mean you won't have any troubles. Sometimes you'll have more! Just remember, the Church is here to help you with them. Okay?"

"Okay."

"Good. Now, how about we should pay another visit to Donna soon, and start planning the wedding ceremony? I'll ask Ottoline to come with us. Don't you think that would be nice? I think it'll be good for Donna to meet one of the other ladies in the church?"

Bertram perked up a bit.

"Not tonight, though," said Clancy. "I don't think my nerves are up to another flight right now. But maybe tomorrow evening? You can tell Donna to expect us..."

"Sure!" gurgled Bertram, happy again, not least at the prospect of going to see his beloved. "You're right, Reverend. You're always right. It'll all work out somehow. I know it will." And off he took.

Left alone, Clancy decided he was starving and went inside the church to explore Grace's wastebasket.

THE FOLLOWING evening's visit to Donna out in the water tower was every bit as nerve-wracking as Clancy's first visit. Donna's mesmerizing presence still had a disturbing effect upon him. He was relieved that Ottoline came along. She seemed to sympathize with Donna's situation and was unaffected by her strangeness. In fact, the two females seemed effortlessly compatible.

Clancy thought of Aunt November and wished that she had had the chance to meet Ottoline. He felt sure that Ottoline could have won her over. Ottoline was so well mannered.

It was Ottoline, as a matter of fact, who explained to Donna the justification behind the concept of a commitment ceremony. "It's helpful, I think, when you are making a big decision, to be in the presence of well-wishers. I only wish that the church had been around when Steven and I began our life together..."

Clancy's ears perked. "Ottoline! That's true! You and Steven aren't married in the Church! We could marry ya'll too!"

Ottoline blinked. She hadn't meant to suggest...in fact, the very idea of taking part was not appealing to her. She opened her beak to protest, but even as she did she realized that she risked putting her foot in it. Had she not just said that she and Steven would have benefited from beginning their life together with the support and blessing of the church?

"Oh, but this is Bertram and Donna's special day..."

"Pssht," said Bertram. "We don't mind, do we, Donna?"

Donna was silent, but lowered her head in a clear gesture of agreement.

"The more the merrier," said Clancy. He'd heard that expression somewhere, and loved it. And in fact the idea of a double ceremony was so appealing to him that he wasn't paying the slightest attention to the fact that Donna wasn't saying much.

"Well, this just tickles me to death. I feel so much better now!" Clancy said this last without thinking.

"Huzzah!" crowed Bertram, out of sheer lust for life.

The little gathering on the water tower access platform went on from there to discuss such mundane details as time, date, and location, as always taking into account the need for discretion. It was determined that a Friday evening, following the departure of the regular AA meeting from the education wing of St. Aloysius Sr., which was often attended by Reverend DeBassompierre himself, would be ideal. The ceremony would take place for sentimental reasons at the birdbath. That settled, the young buzzard, the rat and the pigeon got ready to go back to the church.

Before Clancy straddled Bertram's long thin neck for the return flight, Donna caught his eye, and he approached her, assuming that she wanted to say goodbye or thank you. He recognized that, in spite of her troubles, she was extremely thoughtful.

"Thank you for having us," said Clancy. "It was nice seeing you again."

"You're welcome, of course," she said. "Reverend, could we talk sometime soon?"

She said this last *sotto voce*.

"You mean, you and me?"

"I do," she said. "As soon as possible?"

"Well, sure, Donna ...of course...anytime..."

"Tonight?" she said. "I can come to the church. It will have to be quite late, though..."

"Oh, I don't mind," he said. "Is everything all right?"

"I'd like it to be," she said. "But I will need your help. I'll see you tonight. Bertram says you stay in the cellar?"

"Yes. There's a little wooden door around the corner of the church from where Hertz's composter sits, just tap and wake me up. It's real low to the ground, so..."

"I'll find it," Donna said decidedly. Then, with a voice meant for all to hear, she said, "Thank you all for coming. I'm glad to know you all. Bertram, I'll see you tomorrow."

"Okay," said Bertram. "I'll miss you." And he craned his neck around hers in a sinuous embrace, and then lowered himself so that Clancy could mount. Then they were airborne, with Ottoline right beside them, which helped Clancy feel slightly less afraid.

THE TAP at the crawlspace door came near dawn, and Clancy was ready for it; that is to say, he was awake. He'd slept poorly and fitfully, so curious and apprehensive was he about what Donna might have to say.

He wriggled out of the crack in the corner of the door into the night and greeted her. "Hey, Donna!" he said. "I'd invite you in, but you can see it's a real tight squeeze, and it's a nice night out anyway, not too chilly. If you want, we can take a walk around the church and talk...I have to stick close to my hole here when I'm outside by myself at night but I like to walk around when someone's with me."

"A walk sounds fine," said Donna. "Lead the way."

Clancy, sticking close to the red brick foundation of the church building, began walking towards the front of the church, an area he didn't often get to visit. Donna stepped alongside him and he felt unexpectedly comfortable with her. Her scent—so strong, so much like Bertram's, but with a distinctive briny quality that made it slightly less overpowering—moved along with them.

"So, what would you like to talk with me about, Donna?" he said. "Is it the wedding? The church?"

"Yes and no, Reverend," she said. She looked up towards the stars, as if for a sign of some sort. "It's mainly about Bertram. I do care for him so very much, you know. He *has* been a lifeline for me. But I realize now...I suppose I've known it for a long time and since your last visit I just can't deny it...I can't continue to encourage him. Oh, Reverend...I know he's going to be hurt, but it would be so much worse for him if we..." She stood still, and so did Clancy, as if they were one flesh. "Reverend, what am I going to do?"

Clancy, between the vulture and the foundation of the church, felt a heavy calm settle over himself. He'd known deep down that this was coming. It all made sense now, a terrible but undeniable sense. It had been too good...or rather, too wild to be true...Oh Lord, thought Clancy this isn't going to be pretty.

"Oh Lord," he said aloud, to Donna. "I was afraid of this."

"Were you?"

"I sure was," said Clancy. From where they came to a stop, they could both view the dark, treacherous boulevard that ran before the church property. "He was just too...excited."

Donna expanded slightly, as a creature does when it takes a deep breath. "Yes," she said after a moment. "He's always been so warm and kind, but now there's something...tempestuous about it all. It worries me, Reverend. I'm afraid he's not seeing things as they are..."

Clancy looked out over the treacherous boulevard. He certainly agreed with Donna that Bertram was in over his head, but after all, Donna had not refused his proposal. Had she been careless with his feelings? Wouldn't he have to have felt some encouragement, to become so attached? "Donna, how..." Clancy didn't know exactly how to approach her about her part in creating the problem.

But Donna wasn't dense. "Reverend, I do care for him. I truly never intended for things to go so far. I want more than anything for his dear soul to be happy, and if I believed I could make him happy—in any real and lasting sense—by getting married...I would do anything I could. But Reverend...I know now that it's a losing battle. I could never be for dear Bertram what Ottoline is for her mate, and the other way around...I'm too..." Here she gave a strange little croak. "I'm tired, Reverend. I wouldn't be able to maintain the kind of happiness that could live up to his. I've lost too much, Reverend, you see, I'm so much older, and...do you understand? I would just be a burden ..."

Clancy didn't understand, not really, and yet he knew that the magnificent creature was speaking the truth: between Donna and Bertram, the feelings were powerful and unbalanced, whereas between Ottoline and Steven they seemed to be powerful, yet much simpler and more even. Perhaps that was the point. But wasn't love supposed to overcome any obstacle? He'd heard Reverend DeBassompierre say as much from the pulpit...

"Poor Bertram," was all the rat could think to say.

Donna hung her magnificently ugly, glistening, scabrous head. "I feel responsible," she said. "It's my fault that he's become so devoted. But I was so alone, and he is so delightful. I'm going to miss him very much."

Clancy's impulse, of course, was to console this creature, who was clearly suffering sincere and painful remorse. But how? Oh, Reverend DeBassompierre! He cried out in his mind. What would you do?

"It's not the end of the world," he heard himself saying. The sorrowful vulture lifted her head and regarded him with some surprise and tentative relief. "What do you mean?" she asked.

"I don't know," he said truthfully. "I guess I just think you're doing the right thing, even though it's going to be awful."

༺✦༻

THE RAT and the vulture made their way back to the crawlspace door. They decided, as they strolled, that it would be best for the two of them to talk to Bertram together, to break the news that there was to be no wedding ceremony. Clancy would ask the young buzzard to fly him to the water tower to discuss arrangements with Donna, and once there, Donna and Clancy would then endeavor to help him come to grips with this painful change in plans.

At the crawlspace door Donna paused before taking off. "You are very special, Reverend," she said. "Bertram is lucky to have such a good friend." And she briefly, gently touched the tip of her beak to the hard space between his ears, not unlike a queen dubbing a knight. Before he could respond to assure her that he was a friend to her as well, she was off towards the sunrise.

༺✦༻

IT WAS a scene too painful for Clancy to want to remember or to be able to forget. It was far worse, he thought, than he could have imagined. Bertram was beside himself with fury and misery, and in the end took off into the skies screeching as if possessed.

Donna watched him go. Her expression was blank. After a few moments she remembered Clancy. "Thank you," she said, "for trying. I guess I'll take you home now."

Clancy was wringing his paws with distress. Not even the scene with Bertram's father, with all the spitting and spewing, came close to the unpleasantness of what had just occurred. And it had begun so well. Bertram had agreed to the meeting with pure innocent eagerness; he'd flown low and slow to the water tower, in deference to Clancy's nervousness about being airborne; when they arrived at the water tower he had lovingly craned his long neck around Donna's, for that was their manner of embracing. He'd listened to what Donna had to say at first with incomprehension and then with an agonized rage that made Clancy feel very afraid—for himself, for Donna, and ultimately for Bertram as well. It was as if Bertram's suffering was a thing in itself, and that to simply be in its presence was somehow to be implicated by it. Donna had begun by saying that she treasured their friendship and explaining the reasons for her fondness, pointing out his loyalty, his courage, his kindness, as well as his youthful vigor. She reminded him of the early days of their acquaintance...how they'd encountered one another one day over a carcass, the choicest portions of which Bertram had chivalrously left to Donna in spite of the fact that on sight they'd recognized one another as belonging to opposite factions of their species. She recalled, with sincere emotion, the gentle but swift development of their relationship, from unsanctioned neighborliness to mutual regard, to friendly affection, to loyal devotion, to—at least on Bertram's part—abiding passion. She reminded him of her past, of her exile from her own kind on account of her inability to submit to her first mate's heavy-winged authority, of the loss of her offspring to that ruthless tyrant, her grief and her uncertainty, and her almost constant melancholy. She explained that as much as she loved him, and as grateful as she was that he was so devoted to her, the kind of love he needed from her was just not hers to give on account of her troubles. "Not now," she said. "And I can't say for sure that there will ever be a time when I can say I am capable. There's just too much that I have to make sense of. On my own."

Bertram had at first remained—not calm exactly—but not completely beyond reason. He'd insisted that she was the love of his life and that he would take care of everything for her, that she only needed to trust him.

"I do trust you, Bertram," she said, "And you don't know what it means to me to be able to trust anyone at all. The problem is that I don't trust the future. I don't know that I will ever feel happy again. And that's not fair to you."

"I don't care!" he'd barked. "I love you!" And the contradiction between those two statements seemed not only to escape him, but to enrage him all the more. And it was at that point that he stood, stretched out his impressive wingspan, and let loose with an anguished, gurgling roar. "You promised!" he shouted, and for a moment Clancy was sure that his friend was going to use one of those wings to sweep him off the access platform of the water tower down to his death. Out of sheer instinct, Clancy rushed to Donna's side, so as to be near someone who might save him if he fell. And this self-protective move gave Bertram the wrong impression. "You *whore!*" Bertram croaked, and he charged towards them.

Donna, with the instinct of a thwarted mother, covered Clancy with her wings and ducked beneath Bertram's charge. Bertram did not turn back, but continued off the water tower towards the open sea, leaving Clancy and Donna to regard one another with horror. Things had turned out worse than they could have imagined. It was a perfect storm of misunderstanding.

☙❦☙

WITH NOT A LITTLE uneasy self-consciousness after that disastrous confrontation, Clancy straddled Donna at the base of her
long, featherless neck and held on for dear life for the flight
back down to St. Aloysius. When they landed by the
composter and Donna lowered her head so that he could
dismount, Clancy scrambled off as fast as he could, skittering
over to the crawlspace door so as to put a respectable distance
between himself and her. "Thanks for bringing me back," he
said, rather louder than he would have otherwise. Then, in a
more Clancylike tone, "Oh, I'm so upset! Now he's going to
hate both of us!"

Donna herself was too dismayed to offer comfort. "Poor
Bertram," she said, then spread her wings. "Goodbye, Reverend.
I appreciate your trying to help. But I should have just gone
away." She sprang up and was airborne.

Clancy was then suddenly possessed with great anxiety over
what Donna, in her state of now total abandonment, might do
next. "Donna!" he cried out and up. "I'll fix this! I promise!"

If Donna heard she did not respond, and was soon out of
sight. Clancy remained crouched against the crawlspace door, so
overwrought that he was defecating loosely and noisily to the
amusement of countless young descendants of Hertz who were
regarding him from within the composter.

☙❦☙

TO SAY that Clancy spent a restless night would be an under-
statement. Never in his life had the poor rodent tossed and
turned through such unyielding mental turmoil. He couldn't take
the terribly pastorally mismanaged scene out of his mind's eye,
along with all the things he should have said but didn't. But
worst of all was the recurrent recollection of the fateful moment
when he'd dashed to Donna's side out of sheer cowardice, totally

heedless of how his behavior might be interpreted. Oh, he moaned to himself, I'm just a ninny.

Because there was no other way to understand what he'd done, was there? He'd gotten spooked and scurried for protection like...like a rat! When what he ought to have done was to stand firm, with faith, in the face of Bertram's (after all, very understandable) outburst, and in so doing convey to the buzzard that he, Clancy, would never betray him. But no. He'd panicked instead and now neither Bertram nor Donna would ever come to St. Aloysius Jr. again.

Eventually Clancy just gave up trying to sleep, and out of desperation rather than desire, made his way up the basement stairs into the church proper. His vague intention was to go to the sanctuary and try to pray, but as if with minds of their own his restless legs carried him into the administrative wing, to the office of Reverend DeBassompierre.

It was dark and empty, yet fairly redolent of the usual occupant, whom Clancy so revered as a mentor and an icon of devotion to the study and explication of the Christian faith. How precious were the hours Clancy spent peering at the Reverend from behind the bookcase as he read, wrote, prepared his sermons, and every so often counseled. The Reverend DeBassompierre, especially since he had stopped drinking his beloved Bloody Marys, was so patient, so silently attentive, and so effective when engaged in counseling. Clancy knew that he certainly would have been able to handle the situation with Bertram and Donna with more aplomb. Because, of course, Reverend DeBassompierre was a real Reverend. And I, Clancy said to himself, am just a rat.

This odious comparison was so disheartening that Clancy figured he oughtn't have come to the office, but he couldn't imagine that being anywhere else would make him feel any better, so he stayed. He wandered around a bit, aimlessly, then found himself climbing up into the Reverend's plush leatherette swivel chair behind the desk, and he settled himself into the indent created there by the Reverend's narrow buttocks. He couldn't see much except the space beneath the desk, so he closed his eyes, and after a few moments he began to feel his spirits lighten somewhat. It was comforting somehow to inhabit the space left by the good Reverend's behind. He felt...the only word for it was mercy. As if he was being restored gently to a recognition of his own inexperience. He had no call to expect too much of himself. He was going to make mistakes. The point was to have the courage to fix them. There was no way he could have known that Bertram would lose control in quite the way he had, and Clancy had done what anyone else would have done...he'd gotten out of the way. Never in his wildest dreams would he have imagined that he was giving the appearance that he and Donna were...together.

Clancy began to grind his teeth, a form of self-soothing, as he replayed the terrible scene over again in his mind's eye. But this time he was recalling with conscious intent, so as to learn something new. He put himself in Bertram's place, and saw his pastor and the desire of his heart side by side opposite him, moments after the desire of his heart called off the wedding. Of course the poor buzzard was going to jump to the wrong conclusion. But at the same time, how preposterous! A rat and a buzzard? In love? Surely once Bertram cooled off, he'd realize that there could be nothing between Donna and Clancy.

Was there?

Clancy closed his eyes again. He thought of Donna, how oddly impressive she was, so majestic. It was true that she was stunning to behold. But never in a million years would Clancy want to...would he *long* for her, with all that entailed. No, she was very nice, but so different, as different as Bertram himself, or Ottoline, or Hertz, or the Reverend...

Here he leaped off the Reverend's seat onto the floor, simultaneously leaping off a train of thought that seemed to be heading towards a precipice. He ran out of the office and down to the food pantry, suddenly ravenous. After an entire Little

Debbie snack cake was inside of him he found himself ready to sleep.

৩৯৫৩

THE NEXT DAY, after oversleeping, Clancy was obliged to tell Ottoline what had happened. "Oh dear," she said when the story was done. "What a mess. Oh, poor Donna!"

Donna! Clancy was taken aback, for it seemed to him that Bertram was the one suffering most in the situation. But he held his tongue, because after all, Ottoline always had a way of helping him to see things differently. "She must feel just terrible," the pigeon added.

"I do too," said Clancy. "Oh, Ottoline, now we might never see Bertram again. He hates me. If you could have seen him...I really thought I was going to die."

Ottoline's full breast swelled, then deflated. "I can imagine," she said. "Bertram doesn't know his own strength, I believe. His energy can be overwhelming. That's the real heart of the matter, it seems to me. He hasn't developed a sense of proportion. But he's young, very very young, and his family, I think, has given him too much responsibility and not enough guidance. He'll learn. But in the meantime, it is hard. He certainly needs our sympathy."

Ottoline's words did make sense to Clancy. But her relative placidity, in the face of all that had gone awry, seemed to be missing something. "Oh, Ottoline," he said, "I'm just so afraid he might do something bad."

"Like what?"

Clancy wasn't sure. All he knew was that he was simply afraid. He just knew that something bad was going to happen. "He might...he might..." Clancy reached for his tail. "He was just so...mad!"

"Yes," said Ottoline. "I imagine he was. Jealousy can be very violent." She blinked and lowered her beak to smooth the feathers of her breast. Then she looked at Clancy. "He's in love. Poor child."

Clancy was visited afresh by a spirit of bewilderment. Neither Donna nor Ottoline seemed as alarmed by the change in Bertram as Clancy was. It was as if they'd seen it all before and knew that it was serious, but not necessarily the end of the world.

"Ottoline?" he said. "Should we call off the wedding?"

Ottoline did not hesitate. "Absolutely not," she said. "Steven and I very much want to be married in the church."

❧

CLANCY REMAINED NERVOUS, but he agreed with Ottoline that it was the right thing to do to go on with the ceremony as planned. And there was an additional benefit: making arrangements for the wedding kept his own mind, at least sometimes, off of the mess he'd made of Donna and Bertram's relationship. There were songs to choose, a sermon to prepare, and of course, Ottoline and Steven wanted their many offspring to attend and take part in the ceremony as attendants. It was going to be a major undertaking. Clancy found that he liked making big plans.

On the day of the wedding, early in the afternoon, while Clancy worked hard to commit his short remarks to memory, along with what he could recall of the liturgy in the Book of Common Prayer, a familiar tap, that of a small pointed beak, sounded upon the crawlspace door. "Be right there, Ottoline," he said. "Just a second. I'm practicing my sermon."

He squeezed outside to find that it was Steven, not Ottoline, who had come to call. "Steven!" he said. "What a surprise! Are you ready for your big day?"

Steven, as always a pigeon of few words, simply nodded genially.

"What brings you by, Steven?" said Clancy.

"Nothing," said Steven. "Just visiting." And so saying, he

settled himself onto the dusty ground before the crawlspace and regarded Clancy expectantly. This was disconcerting to the rat, but Clancy was growing accustomed to Steven's rather inscrutable ways. One had to work to get anything out of him, but it was generally worth the effort.

"So how are you feeling, Steven, about the wedding?"

"Not bad."

"Are all your daughters here yet?"

"Oh yeah."

"That's good!"

The conversation fell into a prolonged silence. Clancy was on the verge of ending it by mentioning that he still had some work to do on his sermon, when the taciturn pigeon opened his beak.

"Heard about the trouble with Bert," he said.

Clancy felt his eyes smart a little. "Yes," was all he could manage to say.

Steven went on. "Heard he's gone back to live with his mama and daddy."

"Oh." Clancy was not at all sure he liked the sound of that. But where else was the young buzzard to turn, now that the church had let him down? "Oh, dear," he said, echoing Ottoline.

Steven nodded. "Thought you'd like to know."

"Thanks, Steven." Clancy assumed that the pigeon had finished delivering the news he'd come to pass on. Not for the first time he marveled at the difference between Ottoline and her mate, she so direct and outgoing, he so placid and meandering. How hard it was to imagine them as young pigeons in the throes of passion. I wonder, thought Clancy, if I will ever understand loving.

"We need to keep Bertram in our prayers," he said to Steven, as the mantle of his office as pastor settled upon him, unbidden as if out of thin air, so that all considerations beyond the immediate one, of getting on with the wedding, were relegated to the periphery of his consciousness to wait their turn. "And Donna, too. But for now, we have to focus on you and Ottoline. This is a big step, Steven. Do you realize that?"

"Oh yeah," said Steven mildly.

"Well, good. I know you and Ottoline have always been true to one another, but now you'll be united in the eyes of God, and you'll be an example for all the rest of us. It's going to be a wonderful evening. Let's have a good time. I just hope I can memorize my sermon in time..."

Steven got the hint. "I reckon I'll be off," he said. "See you later, Rev."

"Amen, Steven."

ॐ

"HERTZ? Are you awake? It's me, Clancy! I just wanted to see if you still wanted to come to the wedding. We're going to get started in just a few minutes, out at the birdbath, you know, just like the baptism. A lot has been happening... oh, *so* much...I'll have to tell you all about it later...but anyway, do you want to come? I'm on my way now, and I'm happy to give you a ride..."

Hertz poked his tip out. His initial impulse was to decline as rudely as he could, for he couldn't get over his trepidation at being out in the open around a bunch of birds. But the rat seemed more than usually agitated this night, and it made Hertz curious. "All right," he said, and emerged completely. "But keep those birds away from me."

"Oh, Hertz," Clancy said. "You know no one's going to hurt you. Anyway, you just stick with me." And, arranging the worm across his back in that ancient manner of an ox bearing a yoke, he leaped and scampered onto the floor, down to the basement, out into the churchyard and around to the birdbath. Everyone was there and more, the squirrels, the raccoons, Ottoline and Steve and all their brood, the squirrels, the opossums, also some fireflies. Only Bertram was conspicuously absent. With Hertz still draped across him like a stole, Clancy climbed up onto the lip of the birdbath and raised his front paw in his gesture that was a signal for silence and attention. Then he began, as he'd heard Reverend DeBassompierre begin.

"Dearly Beloved," he squeaked. "We are gathered here tonight to join Ottoline and Steven in the bonds of Holy Matrimony. Now, I know a whole lot of you might wonder, what is the big deal? They've been together for so long, why have a big ceremony? But there's a big difference between being together and being married. And the difference is, Marriage is a blessing from God, and so it changes everything."

Clancy paused, on the one paw for effect...on the other, for a mental breath. He remembered, with some butterflies in his stomach, that very first wedding he ever attended in the sanctuary of St. Aloysius Sr., the marriage of two ladies of that congregation, a situation of which some of the older members of St. Aloysius did not approve. Neither, in fact, had Aunt November. The Reverend DeBassompierre, in his homily, had confronted that disapproval head on. He'd preached that, at one point in his life, he'd shared the view, that Christian marriage was reserved to a union between one man and one woman. But that was before, he said, he'd spent some time in a monastery and taken a trip to Rome, with a good friend who had been raised by two women in a committed monogamous relationship. "My friend," he said, "reminded me that marriage is a transformational event every bit as much as baptism or the other sacraments of the church. And you can't limit transformation to just the status-quo." Clancy wasn't sure what that meant, but he beleived it.

"Ottoline and Steven," Clancy went on, "are on a new journey, a journey that maybe they decided to take together a long time ago, but it has brought them to us, and to this birdbath. From now on, they're going to share everything...not just with each other, but with the Lord. Now, anything that tries to come between them will become a part of what keeps them together." Clancy paused again and thought of how he himself had come between Bertram and Donna, without meaning to. "A wedding reminds us how much we can count on the Lord to stay by our side. The promises that Ottoline and Steven are going to make are the same promises that God makes to us when we let him into our lives. So let's get started, so we can see just how much the Lord loves each and every one of us—even those who aren't here tonight."

Where did that come from, thought Clancy, who had not planned on saying that last sentence. Everyone was waiting, so he shrugged, jostling Hertz a little, and went on. "Anyway," he said. "Ottoline, do you take Steven to be your lawfully wedded spouse, to have and to hold, from this day forward, in sickness and in health, for better or for worse, till death do you part?"

"I do," crooned Ottoline.

"And do you, Steven, take Ottoline to be your lawfully wedded spouse, to have and to hold, from this day forward, in sickness and in health, for better or for worse, till death do you part?"

"I sure do," he said.

"Then with the power vested in me as Reverend of St. Aloysius Jr., I now pronounce you married in the eyes of God. Praise the Lord!"

And with that, the two birds put their tiny heads together, their manner of embracing, and the covenant was sealed, and the gathering around the birdbath erupted in the cheers of many species. Clancy felt exhilarated, somewhat like the feeling he had when he finished his reducing exercises. Ottoline and Steven hopped and fluttered down to the ground and he followed them in a fearless leap and joined the rest of the congregation in congratulating them. After a while they all returned to the compost heap, to continue the celebration in the familiar shelter of the larger church, and Clancy wished, not for the first time, that he had refreshments to offer. But what could he offer to a collection of individual species with such varied diets? It was a quandary that had been on his mind a lot lately. After all, there was more to church than the sermons and the ceremonies. Church members were supposed to share meals and fellowship.

I'll figure something out somehow, he said to himself, as he contentedly watched his flock mingle and chatter all around him. There's got to be something that we can all share.

For the time being, though, he couldn't imagine what that might be. Maybe God would be so kind as to reveal it to him. In the meantime he could only do the best he could to keep St. Aloysius Jr. going.

❧

WHEN THE STARS began to fade, and the wedding party dwindled, Ottoline and Steven, lingering behind, thanked their pastor for a lovely service.

"Such fun," said Ottoline. "I'm only sorry that Bertram wasn't with us."

"He is," said Steven, and, lifting his beak to the sky he pointed to the edge of the woods where, high up in the dense boughs of a towering pine, the shadowed profile of a glowering hook-beaked creature could be seen.

"Lord!" breathed Clancy. "Is that really Bertram?"

"Uh-huh," said Steven. "I believe he's been up there the whole time. Looking."

"Why, Steven, why didn't you tell us!" cried Ottoline.

"Just let him be," Steven advised on his wedding night.

❧

THE NEXT DAY was pleasantly anticlimactic. Life went on as usual, as if nothing much had happened. Clancy took the opportunity that morning to sleep in, to dawdle over his breakfast, to meander in his thoughts. He felt strangely subdued, as if wrapped in an invisible sheet.

Normally he spent the weekdays upstairs, in Reverend

DeBassompierre's office, behind the bookcase, of course, observing, but that morning he felt the need—an unusual need, really, for him—to be out in what was that day a brilliant and clear and gentle morning sunshine. He squeezed himself through the gap in the crawlspace door and crouched for a while, just taking it all in, blinking at first and breathing regularly. He did not particularly want to interact with anyone. Usually, when he didn't feel like talking, it was because he was anxious or upset. But not this bright morning. This morning he simply felt different.

His impulse towards solitude notwithstanding, after a while he rounded the corner of the building and stood by the composter, within reach of its strong stench. He did not call for Hertz, he just stood there and looked out over the playground and the graveyard and woods. Ottoline and Steven were nearby, presumably, probably on their usual power line, and over by the swing set he could see a group of squirrels chasing one another, and he could hear their chittering. Life was going on. Clancy looked up at the sky, clear and cloudless that morning, and a very light yet rich blue color. It seemed to go on forever, above the trees, that endless blue blankness with no sign of sentient life. God was up there, Clancy believed, but not making his presence obvious, having nothing particular to convey at the moment.

Clancy stayed there for a long time, just looking up. He was seeing what he usually missed. And it was lovely, the sunlight, the distant birdsong, even the smell of the compost. He felt as if he could sit there forever and watch the time go by. He supposed he felt the way Reverend DeBassompierre felt at those times at which he, too, stood for long moments at the large window behind his desk, just looking out.

5

CONFIRMATION

I n nine lives she wouldn't dream of catching a rat, much less eating one...though she knew that there were low, gutter, feral types that wouldn't hesitate to subsist in such a manner. She, however, was better bred than that; she was part Manx and thoroughly domesticated. She expected that even the most obtuse rodent would realize that she was too refined to pose a threat; thus, she was not only injured, but also insulted by the fact that she'd been brutally attacked when she had only been trying to introduce herself. The incident had been deeply humiliating—to say the least—and she vowed never again to make the mistake of assuming that wild creatures had any degree of nice perception. After the attack, she'd retreated to the woods to lick her wounds, which were, to be frank, more to her pride than her flesh. But she couldn't stay there long, for the woods are no place for a housecat after dark. Of course, since she'd been evicted, there was no place that was really safe. She had learned by experience that in the daytime it was best for her to stick close to wooded areas, in that there were plenty of trees to climb should a canine or some other mindless predator attempt to overtake her; whereas the yards and avenues and porches and sidewalks of the human habitats tended to be safer at night.

There she would, more often than not, come across some porch with some kibble and milk left out by some kind human soul who perhaps knew what it was like to be a vagabond.

Since becoming homeless her life had become a nightmare with no end in sight. Week after week of living paw to mouth, rummaging through garbage for scraps, dodging and fleeing from more experienced strays, sleeping in snatches under bushes and cars had transformed her into an emaciated, scruffy and flea-bitten shadow of her former sleek self, but at least, she told herself, she still had her pride. She wouldn't sink to the level of her persecutors. She was an aristocrat.

Only in her most desperate moments did it cross her mind that it may well have been her pride that led to her fall. But was it too much to ask to have her seniority taken into account?! She'd done nothing wrong, and it was hardly her fault that the mewling stinking infant that the two humans brought home developed a wheeze and a rash whenever she was nearby! To be relegated to a dark, cluttered garage reeking of gasoline was more than she could bear—she had given them the best years of her life, after all—and so she'd left with the intention never to return. But, of course, she did return, after only a day and a half, only to find that in leaving she'd compromised her position completely. Rather than receiving her back into her rightful home, her former attendants corralled her into a crate, locked her in, and then lifted her into their car. Then they had driven her to a strange fenced-in complex of buildings and bare yards that fairly rang with a cacophony of barks and caterwauls. She was being disowned! Well, she wasn't going to take it lying down! As soon as strange hands reached into the crate for her she scratched and clawed and hissed with such wroth that all hell broke loose. Out of the crate she leaped, onto the landscaped lawn of the animal shelter. Down the driveway and along the highway she scrambled in the direction from which she'd come. But the vehicle had taken so many twists and turns, and she was so sick and dizzy from being caged, that she now saw nothing at all familiar. She went from door to door in the first subdivision she came to, meowing and rubbing up against every human pair of legs she encountered, and sometimes she was given a scrap of something to eat. But that was becoming rarer and rarer. No one wanted to take her in, and after a few days she couldn't blame them, for very soon she looked a fright, as she could see in her reflection in the chrome bumpers and hubcaps of the vehicles she sometimes sheltered beneath. It wasn't long before even her most plaintive mews went unheeded. Then she was reduced to prowling the garbage cans and dumpsters of the restaurants and convenience stores along the boulevard that led to St. Aloysius Church. There, she couldn't help but notice the occasional motley gatherings of wildlife and vermin by the composter. They seemed to be attempting, in the manner of humans, to form some sort of committee. The uncommonly sprightly looking (if overweight) rat appeared to be a particularly inept, if energetic, ringleader. She was not unaware that he'd noted her presence, and with no little suspicion, and by the time he acknowledged her and began to make his way toward her, she was curious enough to meet him halfway. But he'd all of a sudden changed his approach, and attacked her! It really was too much. She'd taken off around the building, and took refuge under a bright red Fiat in the gravel parking lot, to once again nurse her bruised pride and try to figure out where to go next.

CLANCY WAS SPENT FOLLOWING the wedding and the debacle with Donna and Bertram. It had been such a seesaw of emotional ups and downs that he felt he needed to practice a sustained period of self-care. And so for the next few days, he pampered himself by spending long relaxed hours behind the bookcase in Reverend DeBassompierre's office, observing not much more of his mentor's activity than woolgathering and the occasional burst of typing as the human clergyman painstakingly revised his monograph on the pneumatology of St. Methodius of Olympus.

Occasionally—well, quite rarely, actually—Reverend DeBassompierre did take a call, rather than leave it for Grace to handle. Clancy always enjoyed hearing the Reverend on the phone, even though the conversations were rarely anything to do with ministry. Grace handled most of the day-to-day pastoral concerns, as Reverend DeBassompierre felt himself more adept at crisis counseling.

Hence, whenever the reverend normally accepted a call, Clancy could always presume that it was one of three possible callers: the bishop, the Reverend's editor, or the Reverend's mother. It was instructive to note that the young Reverend seemed to respond in a distinct manner towards each of these three callers: eager to please with the Bishop, unyielding yet grateful with the editor, and long-suffering with his mother.

And so it came as some surprise when, one afternoon not long after the wedding, Clancy heard Grace buzz the Reverend and ask him if he was available to take a call from a Reverend Norris. "Who?" asked Reverend DeBassompierre with not a little irritation, for he had been dozing.

"A Reverend Norris," said Grace. "George Norris."

The sudden shift not only in the Reverend's expression, but in the very atmosphere of the office, was marked. It was as if a window had opened, admitting sunshine and fresh air. "George!" cried the Reverend, with more pleasure than Clancy had ever heard him express. "Of course! Put him through! Thank you, Grace."

Clancy did not have to see to picture the astonishment on Grace's own face, for although she knew she was appreciated, she was never thanked. "Hold on..." she said, with uncharacteristic softness.

"George!" the Reverend DeBassompierre cried into the telephone receiver. "How are you!"

The voice on the other end was nothing of course but an

inarticulate buzz to Clancy, but the Reverend's rare smile didn't fade. "Oh, no no," the Reverend said. "Not a bad time at all...no, just going over some notes for the Methodius piece. What's going on with you?"

More inarticulate buzzing. Clancy wished, not for the first time, that his hiding place were closer to the Reverend's desk.

"George! You're joking! That's wonderful! Congratulations! Mazel Tov!" The Reverend's voice and tone were still hearty, but his wide smile began to wilt. "Of course," he said. "I'd be honored. Just let me know the time and place as soon as you can, so I can have Grace move things around for it. I don't suppose you're interested in having the wedding here...?"

"I know. Of course. Just kidding. I agree...and besides, it'll be a nice trip for me; I haven't been back to Cambridge since we graduated! Hard to believe. It'll be fantastic. I'll get in touch with the monks and see if there might be room in the guesthouse. Tell Phillipa I'm all in. And of course, pass on my congratulations to her. Now...have you thought about music? Are you going to have a nuptial mass?"

There was a sustained series of buzzings on the other end, during which the Reverend did not say much, but rather nodded a lot, with the edge of his free hand against his brow, casting a shadow over his eyes. Clancy was curious beyond endurance. He did not know who this George person was, but the Reverend's at first buoyant and then subtly deflated expression told him that it was someone that Reverend DeBassompierre had very different feelings for than he had for the bishop, the publisher or his mother.

As if he knew...though of course he could not possibly have known...that he was being observed, the Reverend swiveled around in his desk chair to face the window behind his desk, stretching the curly cord of the telephone. Now Clancy could only see his mentor's face as a silhouette.

"Me?" the Reverend said after a while. "Oh, you know me. Not much going on in that department, I'm afraid. I guess I'm too much of a workaholic to have much of a social life these days. On top of the presentation at the SBL, I'm working on a little article about John Chrysostom for the AAR, and of course there's the proofs for my monograph. And the parish work. Oh! I guess there is one new wrinkle—I've adopted!!"

A clear squawk and some excited buzzing from the other end. Clancy saw the Reverend's brow lift and lower. "Ha ha," he said. "No, not that kind of adoption. No, I've just taken in a stray cat...or, rather, she's taken me. She crawled underneath my car right here at the Church just a couple of weeks ago..."

Clancy's every whisker, every strand of his fur, and even his tail stiffened. Just the mention of the word that signified that beast was enough to set his teeth on edge. He only barely held in a squeal.

"I know, I know..." the Reverend was saying. "Believe me, I certainly wasn't planning on taking over any more responsibilities than I already have...but I'd say it was preordained! She didn't exactly follow me home, but she certainly followed me into my car, and she wouldn't move even when I started the ignition, and believe it or not, she was a perfect angel for the entire ride...you know how cats are sometimes when you relocate them. Anyway, that's what's been going on down here in the swamps..."

The Reverend paused to allow for a bit of buzz from the other end.

"No...there wasn't any collar, no chip, nothing. As a matter of fact, she looked pretty mangy; I could tell she'd been out on her own for a while. Probably weeks. But I took her to a vet near the church and got her checked out and cleaned up, and now she actually looks pretty good! She's obviously been neglected, and she still looks underweight, but since she's been in the condo with me I've been able to see that at least at some point she had a decent home. She's finicky about her food...won't eat any meat other than fish, if you please, and she sleeps on my grandmother's velveteen throw pillow. Of course she's litter trained, and she's been spayed, which is a real relief. I guess we're soul mates..." The Reverend seemed jarred by this juxtaposition of thoughts, for he swung back around to the desk and leaned forward. "At any rate, it's nice to have something to go home to after work these days..." The Reverend closed his eyes, as if in silent prayer. There was a brief buzz from his friend on the other end.

"What? Oh! Yes...you'll like this...I named her Macrina. After...of course, of course. I knew *you'd* understand..."

The rest of the one-sided conversation was brief and unremarkable, and at any rate, it was lost on Clancy, who was so upset that he could not hear a word over the rush and throb of his own accelerated heartbeat. That cat!! That horrible, hateful, vicious and godless predator! Taken in by the Reverend himself! Into his home no less! It was an abomination! Clancy thought he might explode with the intensity of the umbrage he was feeling. As it was he couldn't help unloading a copious amount of loose stool behind the bookcase.

🐀

MACRINA, as she now regarded herself, perched on the dinette counter of the Reverend DeBassompierre's split-level townhome and surveyed her new domain. It was nothing fancy, but it was decent. She considered herself to have been thoroughly vindicated. She hadn't dared to hope that things could work out so well for her in the end. She glanced sideways to get another glimpse of herself in the aluminum casing of the toaster on the counter. She was still too underweight, but her coat was clean, well brushed and regaining its former gloss, and her eyes were bright and clear. The nice young clergyman who rescued her had just a few days before, on Monday, which seemed to be his day off, taken her to a facility to be given a checkup and grooming. If anything, she looked better than she ever had, for her former owners had forced her to wear an extremely tacky leopard print collar.

She closed her eyes, twitched her ears, and curled into a comfortable napping curve. She had, she felt, a lot of rest still to catch up on. For, although the days since her rescue had been a great relief—infinitely less harrowing than the weeks (and maybe even the entire remembered lifetime) that preceded them—they had nonetheless been exhausting. It was not easy acclimating oneself to a new way of life, even when such a change was infinitely for the better. It was only now that her new keeper had returned to his office at the church for the day, that she felt at leisure to ponder her reversal of fortune.

It alarmed her not a little to think how thoroughly she had been led by sheer desperate instinct. The fact was that, more than anything else, she had allowed herself to be taken in on account of the young clergyman's shoes. Clean, carefully polished and clearly well-made, they captivated her attention when, underneath the little sports car, she saw them approaching. Then, just as she was tensing her body into a crouch in order to dash away in the opposite direction, the shoes came to a stop some distance ahead, and a human face appeared, upside down and at an angle, to regard her. It was a male face, very much unlike and instantly preferable to the youngish, florid, full-bearded and compulsively chuckling face of the male half of the couple that had formerly kept her. This upside down face was clean-shaven and it possessed, even in its awkward position, a solemnity that she experienced as sobriety. This was the face of a person who, although young, had some degree of self-possession, and was obviously attentive to its surroundings, for, having sensed her presence beneath the vehicle it was approaching, came to a stop and investigated, and then did not take any sudden histrionic action.

And so, having taken the measure, albeit unconsciously, of that calm, well-groomed face, she intuited that it meant her no harm. It was, in fact, a face that radiated intelligence. It lifted itself out of her view, and the nicely polished shoes stepped forward, but slowly. She readied herself for flight, but only in the event that she had to, and emerged toward the shoes from underneath the vehicle, lowered her haunches to assume the classic position of cautious acceptance, and looked up at the astonished but still reserved expression of a youngish male human who wore a curious tabbed collar.

Astonished the expression definitely was, but there was no tsking of the tongue, no hissing command to scat or scram as she'd heard lately from so many humans, no callous kicks towards her, no untoward reaction whatsoever. Just a steady, thoughtful look and a question spoken in the plain English she was familiar with—"Where did you come from?"—articulated as normally and as devoid of over affectionate condescension as if the human were speaking to a fellow adult of his own species.

Her only response was to blink. The tall, slim figure before her bent its knees and leaned forward and lowered its brow in a diagnostic expression. "No collar," it muttered to itself, for the tacky leopard print collar had been removed before her arrival at the shelter. "Half-starved. Now what kind of person would let a cat like this loose without a collar! I swear to God, this kind of wanton irresponsible thoughtlessness is going to make a double predestinarian of me yet. Just disgraceful."

The clergyman stood and crossed his arms and continued to gaze down at her with a thoughtful, serious expression. One hand lifted, after a while, and rested its fingertips against a hollow, clean-shaven cheek. "Hmmm," it said again. Then it inhaled and exhaled slowly, as if to extract some vital element from within the air. "All right," the human said, whether to himself, to her, or to some invisible entity. He reached over and opened the door of the Fiat, then stepped back, hands on hips. The clergyman regarded the cat, and the cat the clergyman. After a moment, during which both creatures measured their breaths, she turned and climbed into the backseat of the vehicle, and rested her chin upon her front paws, looked out at the clergyman and waited.

The clergyman was surprised, but not inordinately so. For

most of his life he'd felt a mild affinity for cats...such mysterious, self-sufficient, yet companionable creatures they were, requiring, unlike humans, little to entertain them. But his mother, professing allergies, had never allowed one in the house.

"Well, hello!" he said. "You're pretty presumptuous." He stood for a long time, looking at the scruffy, yet somehow composed creature that had settled in the attitude of a sphinx on his back seat. He could not suppress a tiny smile.

"I seem to have picked up a hitchhiker," he said aloud. He leaned into the backseat, put out his right hand, and stroked the animal's hard little head with one long finger. The cat closed its eyes, something in the manner of a prelate accepting an act of obeisance. "Hmmm," said the clergyman again, standing up straight. "Interesting. What would Jesus do?"

Hands on his hips, he looked up into the blue late afternoon sky and seemed to be searching it for some message. After a moment of this he shrugged and folded his long body into the driver's seat.

He drove the short, convoluted distance to his townhouse complex on the edge of town, and every few moments he would glance at his backseat passenger in the rearview mirror. The cat, for her part, remained composed, though, as always when she was in a moving vehicle, she felt as if she was being internally rearranged. But the uncomfortable journey ended soon enough. The clergyman pulled the Fiat into a parking space in front of a row of slim townhomes, the exteriors of which were not a little shabby and in need of new siding. He cut the ignition and looked one more time at the reflection of the cat. "Here we are," he said. "There's no place like home."

He opened the driver's side door, stepped out, and leaned into the backseat. "Here goes nothing," he said obscurely, and he held out his arms.

She stood, she stretched, she lowered her gaze, not in submission, but assent. Clean hands with pared nails emerged from starched white cuffs, cupped her beneath her tail and around the abdomen, and lifted her out of the Fiat, holding her loosely against a broad flat chest before settling her into the crook of one arm. "Interesting," murmured the priest, who then bore her up the four stairs of his stoop and into his home.

As soon as the door closed behind them, he set her down on the carpeted foyer floor. Immediately she made her way up a series of stairs into the kitchen directly above and ahead, drawn by the afternoon sunshine streaming in through the small window above the kitchen sink. This was a half-conscious test of the young clergyman's mettle. Even before the catastrophe, she had never felt welcome in certain parts of the couple's home, among them the kitchen, which was considered sacrosanct to the young woman's catering 'side gig,' as she called it with an air of false self-deprecation.

The clergyman made no protest, no 'scat,' or 'psst,' or 'no, no!' He just followed her, then stood leaning against the doorsill while she leaped up onto the dinette counter that separated the kitchen from the living room and turned her head to regard him. "I guess you're hungry," he said sensibly. "I'll be back."

He went into another room, returned in another outfit, and went out the front door. So she took the opportunity to look around, to see what she'd gotten herself into. There was not a lot to see. This habitat was in many ways very different from her former, much larger, much more contemporary suburban abode. Though clean, the living room here was cluttered, books and papers everywhere, in random places on the floor, stacked upon the cushions of the sofa, stacked high upon the coffee table, and a set of shelves against the wall was stuffed with books. There was an old console television set, but no gaming console, such as the male half of the couple she had formerly depended upon, had constantly involved himself with. There was a set of sliding glass doors that led to a small concrete-floored and wooden-railed balcony that overlooked a narrow strip of grass and looked right into the woods that seemed to be invisibly and inexorably approaching the building.

Across the room from the dinette, an opening led down a short dark and bare hallway. To the right was a tiny full bath, and at the end of the hall and to the left was one lone bedroom. This room was dim, admitting a late afternoon light, muted and begreened by the woods close by through a large uncurtained second story window. The bed was full-sized and unmade, a heap of sheets and a comforter at its foot. A small wooden crucifix was nailed to the wall above the headboard. Beside the bed there was a nightstand with a shadeless lamp and a leaning tower of hardback books. There was a tall, dark dresser opposite the bed with pictures in standing frames on top; these were all images of human faces. She left the bedroom and returned to the bright kitchen.

With an effortless leap upward, she settled back onto the dinette counter next to the ornamental fruit bowl. She waited, pondering her impressions. These were very close quarters. And yet, something about the place gave her the sense that there would be more room for her and her delicate nervous system then there had been in the much larger and more contemporary suburban single family home. Her former keepers, who had together operated a graphic design business from that home, were always talking, if not to one another, then to and through their many electronic devices—that is, when they weren't huddled together before a screen, typing and scrolling and pointing and clicking and cutting and pasting and peering and pursing in an activity they referred to as 'content creation.' The atmosphere was at all times, even in the still of the night when the couple was ostensibly at rest, frenetically eager. It was as if the very air was tainted by their utterly unconscious insecurity. It was this lack of self-awareness that had led to their decision to bring first a housecat, and then a child, into their distracted lives, never for a moment considering that they were only equipped *financially* to take on responsibility for another being; in their capacity to provide attention to a creature any less self-sufficient than a cat, they were as barren as dust. The male half of the couple was particularly unconsciously self-absorbed. With the ginger-colored beard he compulsively stroked and his fashionably unfashionable eyeglasses, he gave the impression of being perpetually in character, and in the character of a character. He was given to unnaturally hearty bursts of laughter but his jollity waxed and waned in tandem with his supply of marijuana. The cat had only put up with them as long as she had because they so frequently were away for days at a time on camping trips, during which she was cared for and left alone by a part-time housekeeper.

This small, cluttered apartment could certainly use a part-time housekeeper, but it did not matter; she rather liked it. The closeness of those dense woods to the west windows gave it a fortress-like quality that appealed to her, and the dust on the surfaces and the stacks of books and piles of papers suggested a degree of unselfconsciousness on the part of the inhabitant—an unselfconsciousness at least in regard to appearances—that boded well. There was an atmosphere of quiet determination, of focus, and there is nothing more salutary to the feline nervous system than focus. It is, after all, what makes the world go round.

She rested her chin on her paws and attended to the steady hum of the refrigerator, one of her favorite sounds, which recalled to her in a pleasantly haunting way her long forgotten kittenhood. She had drifted, by relaxing her own will, into a light, refreshing slumber, when the sound of steadily approaching human footsteps alerted her to the fact that the clergyman had returned.

He entered with a large paper bag, set it upon one of the dinette stools, and preceded to unpack it. First, he pulled out a slim, silvery band, which after a moment she recognized as a collar. He placed it on the counter before her as if to communicate that he would not be refused. "I went to the Pet Mart," he said. "And to the supermarket. For supplies. Now, first things first. You are going to have to wear this collar, like it or not. I don't know if you had one before, but it is going to be one of the rules of this house, that all inhabitants possess proper identification in case of emergency. If, God forbid, something happens and you get out and get lost, I had a little tag made so that anyone who finds you can contact me. And...by the way...I've taken the liberty of giving you a name. I don't know what you might have been called before, or how you might refer to yourself, if at all, but I'm going to call you Macrina. Think of it as your Confirmation name. Macrina is the name of a very pious and wise woman of the early Christian patristic period, and in the Eastern Rite Churches she's considered to be an important and authoritative saint. Her name— and yours—is engraved on the tag, along with my name and my contact information. Now...hold still..." And he buckled the thin silver strap beneath her chin swiftly and deftly. She had decided beforehand not to interfere. The slim silver band wasn't the most comfortable article in the world. Left to her own, she would do without a collar, period. But at least this collar was less gaudy and gauche than the other one. She stretched and shook her head several times to settle the thing as loosely as possible against her fur, and the clergyman watched her attentively for any indication of discomfort. Seeing none, he reached again into the bag.

"I don't know what your taste in food is," he said, "so...at least to begin with, I got an assortment. Something tells me you have pretty fastidious tastes. Also—" he reached into the bag and heaved out a smaller bag, clear plastic and exuding the familiar chalky scent of fresh litter—"I trust all the saints that you've been housetrained." He arched an eyebrow. "If not, you are going to want to be a fast learner. This place is no penthouse, but I want it to at least smell clean. I can't stand an inconsiderate roommate...and believe me, I've had my share of those."

He reached back into the bag, pulled out a large grey blue plastic rectangular tub, and set it down in an alcove off the kitchen, wherein stood a stacked washer-dryer set. "There. There's your WC. Your loo." He looked pleased when he turned back to the dinette, as if something had fallen into place within him. "Now. How about supper?"

He crossed the floor, reached up above the kitchen counter into a presswood cabinet, and brought out a short stack of three china bowls. He sat one before her, opened one of the cans of food—tuna, by the smell of it—and emptied it into the bowl. One other bowl he filled with about an inch of milk from a large carton that he lifted out of the bag.

Then he settled himself on a dinette stool, reached back into the bag, and pulled out a smaller plastic bag. Out of that he withdrew two small white cartons, one filled with rice, the other with stir fry vegetables, and these he emptied into the remaining china bowl. Together they dined, with the homey hum of the refrigerator adding texture to the silence, and a buffer to what would otherwise be the unpleasant sound of human chewing, and when the meals were finished, the Reverend removed the bowls and placed them in the sink. He then settled himself on the sofa in the living room, and spread several books of varying thickness open before him on the coffee table. And he alternately read and wrote for the next couple of hours. The cat, who now thought quite naturally of herself as a creature named Macrina, spent a few minutes after her supper licking her chops and paws, before settling herself on the sofa beside (but at a respectful distance from) the Reverend as he studied. Thus a routine was established. It was Sunday night.

☙❧

FROM THAT POINT FORWARD, Macrina spent most of her time alone, which suited her perfectly, for she was spayed, after all, and so not prone to any urge for intimacy; and even apart from that, she had always tended to need her space. That said, she was generally pleased to see her personable and solicitous new human when he came back to the townhouse from his work at the church. She didn't mind, as she'd minded with her former

keepers, that he indulged in the sentimental and somewhat frus-
tration-inducing practice of talking to her, for at least he spoke
to her as a peer, and not as one would speak to a creature of
lower intelligence. "Good morning, Macrina," he grumbled every
morning when she awakened him at dawn for her morning meal,
after which he would sit up and mutter a morning prayer. And
when the two of them dined together in the evenings at the
dinette counter he often vocalized to her the thoughts on his
mind, unbosoming himself of his fears and desires, so that she
developed a sense of what it was like to be a human, albeit of a
peculiar, solitary sort.

"I'm in a rut, Macrina," he sighed one evening while picking
at a Caesar salad. "The church is stagnating. No new members in
over six months now. The adult education program hasn't gotten
off the ground, and if it weren't for Grace taking the lion's share
of counseling sessions, I wouldn't have anything to show for us."
He then stood and went to the humming refrigerator and
returned to the counter with a carton of ice cream. Comfort
food, he called it. "And if it was just the church in limbo that
would be bad enough, but...oh, my whole damn life is on hold.
I'm pushing 35, Macrina, and look at me! Sure, I'm finally getting
some attention for my book, but it certainly isn't bringing in any
seminary job offers. I'm telling you, I don't know how much
longer I can stand doing parish work. I was feeling okay about it
all, though, until I heard from George. Of course I'm glad for
him, that he's finally found someone and he's getting married.
But it always seems like everyone's moving forward except me..."

The long-faced human took several heaping spoonfuls of ice
cream into himself and then pushed the carton to the other side
of the dinette counter. "Gross. I'm indulging in self-pity and high
fructose corn syrup. I guess it's time to make another appoint-
ment with Sr. Albertine." The young priest sighed and looked at
the cat with a sad warm half-smile. "Although you're pretty good
at active listening. Maybe *you* should be my spiritual director!"

Macrina had no idea what the young priest was talking about,

but she did sense that he was paying her a rather high compli-
ment. And she did know what it felt like to be abandoned.

She hopped off of the dinette counter, took a moment to
clean her chops and paws, rubbed the length of herself against
the priest's pant leg, then stepped around and into the living
room on the other side of the dinette. With a pointed glance
back at the somewhat bemused priest, she hopped up onto the
sofa and came to rest in the spot she normally occupied when he
spent the evening with his books and papers.

The young priest laughed a rare laugh. "All right," he said.
"Point taken. Enough self-pity. I always have my work to do."
And he put his ice cream back in the freezer and joined her on
the sofa.

❧ 6 ❧

PENANCE

It was a beautiful clear sparkling Sunday morning, and even though it was not yet spring, the churchyard had an Easterly air on account of the pastel quality of the sun and sky and grass. The bells of the First Presbyterian Church down the boulevard began the call to worship at ten in the morning, and so the congregation of St. Aloysius Jr. gathered, as was their custom, around the composter. Ottoline was particularly excited about this morning's service, for she had made the acquaintance earlier in the weekend, of a family of geese who had recently taken up residence around the man-made pond of a nearby office park, and she'd invited them to attend.

When the geese arrived, walking boldly and in single file across the boulevard, impervious to the honking cars they passed in front of, Ottoline greeted them with warmth, but asked them in the future to be a bit more discreet with their arrival. "We don't want to attract undue attention from the humans," she explained.

"Why not?" said the father goose. "They don't own the world, even though they think they do."

"Well, I think they do own this particular property," said

Ottoline. "But at any rate, I'm glad you could all join us. Let me introduce you..." And she dutifully make the rounds with the geese in tow, acquainting them with the squirrels, with Hertz, the raccoons, and afterwards explaining that on account of some problems at home, one of the most active members of the congregation, a buzzard by the name of Bertram could not attend that weekend. "But I hope you'll have the opportunity to meet him soon. And of course you know my husband Steven, and as for the Reverend...well, he seems to be running a bit late. I'll just go check in on him. Excuse me..."

She hurried over—on foot—to the crawlspace door and tapped. "Reverend?" she cooed. "Is everything all right? It's time for church...Didn't you hear the bell?" She was careful not to allow consternation or irritation to creep into her tone. She waited for more than a moment, but then, hearing no response, she tapped again. "Reverend!" she cooed with more urgency. "Reverend! Are you all right? Everyone's waiting, Reverend, gathered at the composter. And Reverend, there's a new family visiting, I believe their vacationing from Canada. Geese, of all things, and a bit forward, as northerners can be, but they seem pleasant enough, and I think they would be an interesting addition to the congregation..."

No response.

"Reverend, please! Can't you hear me? If you can, please answer me!"

She lowered her head and peered into the gap at the bottom of the crawlspace door, but she couldn't see anything but the darkness within. "Reverend!" she called again, and this time with all the volume that mounting concern called for. "Reverend, please answer me! I'm getting worried! Reverend, if you can hear me, you must answer, or I'll have to...I'll just have to come in there..."

Ottoline waited. She had a feeling that her last statement would elicit a response. She was not incorrect. After a moment she heard a muffled movement from within. Then came the Reverend's voice, thick with sleep. "I'm fine," he said. Then, as if there was no contradiction whatsoever, he added, "I can't preach, I don't feel well."

"What's wrong?!"

"Nothing." Thus came another wild contradiction, at once forceful and petulant. "I'm fine."

"Reverend! You're not making any sense! I'm getting Steven..."

Clancy was wrapped up in his mildewed choir robe bedding, so his cry was muffled but intelligible. "No!" the rodent said. "Just leave me alone. If you want to have church, do it yourself. Everyone likes you better than they like me anyway. I quit."

Ottoline felt as stunned as if she'd crashed in flight up against a plate glass window. She knew the wedding had taken a toll, especially on account of the misunderstanding with Bertram, which still had not been cleared up, but never in the world would she have expected this from the Reverend! She stepped away from the crawlspace and turned to regard the gathering around the composter. On account of the geese, the congregation was larger than it had ever been before, Bertram's conspicuous absence notwithstanding. In his usual state of mind Clancy would be thrilled, would jump at the chance to welcome the new potential parishioners. Something was very, very wrong. What could it be?

The gathering at the composter was becoming clearly restless; many of the creatures, including Steven, were now regarding her curiously. Ottoline's heart sank. She was as certain of what she must do as she was reluctant to do it. For the church to go without a Sunday service at this crucial point in its growth would set a disastrous precedent. Now more than ever, dedication and commitment were key. Whatever was troubling the Reverend would only be made worse in the long run if she didn't step up. Oh Reverend, she warbled to herself, don't do this to me.

"Reverend, please..."

"LEAVE ME ALONE!"

Ottoline's bosom doubled in size with indignation. How rude! Whatever was bothering the Reverend; there was no reason for him to shout at her! Not for the first or last time she thought witheringly of the earthworm that the Reverend set such store by. He was, as far as she was concerned, a bad influence. But there was no time to argue.

She leaped into a short flight to land on top of the composter.

"The Lord be with you," she cooed. "I'm sorry to have to report that the Reverend is indisposed. He's asked me to lead the service this Sunday. So, I suppose, to begin, I'll ask my husband, Steven, to please lead us in the opening hymn...*Softly and Tenderly, Jesus is Calling.*

And so the church rolled on.

WRAPPED UP IN HIS BEDDING, Clancy heard Steven singing, and he felt such an uncomfortable mélange of resentment and relief that he nearly cried out as if suffering a physical pain. Part of him was glad that Ottoline cared enough, and could be counted on, to keep the church going in his absence. Part of him felt betrayed, as the church was his God-given vision, not hers. What did it mean if there could be church without him? It meant that he was not so important after all. Not to Reverend DeBassompierre, and not to his own parishioners. He put the end of his tail in his mouth and began to gnaw, at first tentatively, and then with vigor, until he could taste the hard dark taste of his own blood. Dimly, through the folds of his bedding, he could hear the soft warbles of Ottoline's preaching. He couldn't make out what she was saying, and he didn't want to. He felt sure that whatever she was saying was smarter than anything he might have said. He might as well face it. The church didn't need him. No one did.

Clancy's sharp-edged incisors pierced the tough skin of his tail and touched a nerve. He squealed in anguish so loudly that his own ears rang.

❦

OTTOLINE LED the service as best she could, and only hoped that she hadn't made a mistake. It was for her an ordeal. First of all she had to come up with some explanation for the suddenness of the Reverend's absence. Then, what was worse, she was obliged to deliver a sermon, and this without the slightest idea of what the Scriptures of the day were supposed to be. She kept it short and sweet, and, as if she were giving advice in a private conversation with one of her grown daughters, she spoke upon the importance of keeping one's temper when faced with a situation in which a loved one has decided to be foolish and or stubborn. Surely, she told herself, there must be something in the Bible about that.

And there was the family of geese. She approached them immediately following the closing hymn, before they could walk away.

"I'm so sorry," she said. "This was unexpected, to say the least. But our Reverend, who is usually in excellent health, has been fighting off a digestive complaint, which seems to have gotten the better of him. He's been working so hard lately, the poor fellow, I'm just grateful that I could step in..."

"Doesn't make any difference to me," said the father goose, before the pleasant-looking mother goose could say one word. "So you say you have these meetings every week?"

"Yes, generally," said Ottoline. "And on special occasions."

"And what for?"

Ottoline was taken aback. Wasn't it plain from what this

goose had just participated in that the reason for coming together for a regular worship service was for mutual support and to share the experience of gratitude for life? She wished the Reverend were there to explain. "I suppose to show appreciation to the Creator of all that we see and experience..."

"To who?"

Ottoline, aware that her own sense of the divine was very vague, again wished that the Reverend would get himself together and come out and take over this conversation. She could only hope that she wasn't saying anything incorrect. She decided to sidestep the question.

"...And to share fellowship. As you can see, we are a very diverse and open community, and we would love for you to join us regularly for as long as you're in the area..."

"Don't know if I see the point. I don't see where anyone's given me anything I haven't worked for..." And as if the very concept of Providence was an affront to his authority, he made a motion with his neck and beak that seemed to signal a command to his brood to line up behind him.

"Well, I'm not an expert on these matters," Ottoline said feebly, once again terribly aware of her lack of theological training. "But I think you'd enjoy speaking to our Reverend about these questions. He's studied the scriptures thoroughly. He is an ordained minister, after all." She glanced toward the cellar of the church. "I'm sure that next Sunday he'll be all better, and I know he'll be thrilled to answer any questions that you...or your lovely family...might have about our church and its beliefs. In the meantime, won't you stay awhile and meet some of our members? Let me introduce you first to my spouse, Steven..."

When the fellowship hour ended, Ottoline was so frazzled that she felt she had to have time to herself. She flew herself to the top of the Burger King sign down the boulevard and perched there for a long while, smoothing her ruffled feathers and taking in the breeze from the nearby sea, until her nerves were settled.

⚜

CLANCY WOKE up in a cold sweat from a dream as terrible as it was terribly exciting. He was so disoriented that for a moment he was sure that Aunt November was still alive, sharing the cellar with him, and he was terrified at the possibility that he might have betrayed some secret in his sleep. For he woke up all entangled in the discarded choir robe, panting and sweating, and with every muscle straining and his little heart throbbing a mile a minute and his tail as stiff as a sword. Only after a long, horrible moment of feeling obscurely surveilled and shamed did he come back to the present.

Remnants of the dream surfaced like corpses in a flood, and his damp fur stiffened with the still palpable feeling that he was being chased into a dark corner and dwarfed by some overarching presence that was about to devour him without mercy. Alongside the horror, there was a mounting and desperate exhilaration. The overpowering presence had something of the essence of Reverend DeBassompierre, looming, human and austere and yet there was also something of that awful cat, crafty and wild. It was as if the two beings were one...savior and destroyer, mentor and nemesis. The worst thing about the dream was that there was that element of excitement—a helpless yet headstrong abandonment of all restraint, a triumph of incontinence. He felt spent and defeated. It was hideous.

Clancy wriggled himself out of his tangle of choir robes, clammy now with his own sweat, and his eye was drawn inexorably to the irregular chink of bright, brash daylight shining through that gap at the bottom of the crawlspace. The cellar of the church, with its shadows, its dampness, its disorder and the constant odor of mildew and rat droppings now seemed haunted by dark suggestions of abasement. The pun, of course, escaped him. He squeezed himself through the gap into temporarily dazzling daylight. While his eyes adjusted he took a deep breath, catching a whiff of the compost, and this reminded him that his oldest friend, who knew him better than he knew himself, was near.

And Clancy placed his brow against the casing of the composter as if it were the Wailing Wall.

"Oh Hertz!" he moaned, scarcely aware of what he was saying. "Hertz, I need your help...I don't know what's wrong with me!" He felt his heart begin to race again, and he reached for his tail, put it in his mouth, and gnawed and waited. While he waited, he looked around, and was relieved that there did not seem to be any parishioners nearby. They were all, he imagined, going about their own fulfilling lives while he suffered. It just wasn't fair.

Hertz took his time deciding whether or not to respond. Clancy had a history of getting all excited over nothing; in fact, as far as Hertz was concerned, this was the rodent's defining characteristic. And yet this time it seemed different. Hertz had never before known the rat to express self-doubt. He poked out his tip, just a sliver.

"Oh Hertz! There you are! Oh, I've got to talk to you. Hertz, I just want to... I don't know what I want to do. I feel like nothing matters anymore." And hearing so plainly, in his own voice, the essence of how he felt, Clancy now suddenly experienced a cold and terrible despair unlike anything he'd ever felt before.

Hertz, who rarely felt as if anything mattered, nonetheless was mildly alarmed. It was certainly characteristic of the rat to get himself all in a tizzy over nothing, but he wasn't sure he was comfortable with Clancy being conscious of the emptiness and absurdity of existence. He didn't think the big ninny could handle it. "Well Good Ground!" The worm made a rare effort not to be dismissive. "Get ahold of yourself! It isn't the end of the world, is it? What the hell is wrong?"

"Oh, Hertz!" Clancy wailed. "It *is* the end of the world. At

least it feels like it to me! It's Reverend DeBassompierre, he..."
And Clancy reached for his tail and began to wring and twist it
in between his two front paws.

"Stop that!" said Hertz. "You *know* it makes me nervous when
you do that! Put your stinking tail down and look at me. What
happened to that Reverend DeBassoon of yours. Don't tell me
he's *dead*..."

"Oh Hertz! No, he's not dead. Oh God no! Thank the Lord
it's nothing like that." But even as he said this he could not deny
that he would probably feel better... at least a little...if the
Reverend had died. This realization made him feel all the more
evil. He couldn't bear himself. He reached for his tail, remembered Hertz's admonition, and let it drop to the ground.

"He's not dead," Clancy said again, this time in a manner
unrecognizable to him as himself, so calm and flat it made his
normally high-pitched and excitable voice sound. And then it
was as if the calm flatness of his voice descended upon him, and
he felt calm and flat and lifeless, like a frozen puddle. "He's got
that cat." And he could not stop himself from adding, "that
damned cat."

Hertz was himself rather chilled by the rodent's sudden and
unfamiliar new tone. One of the worm's many descendants
wriggled through one of the vent openings nearby to see what
was happening, and Hertz hissed at the youngster sharply to go
back inside and mind its own business. Clancy didn't seem to
even notice. Hertz spoke next with what was for him
gentleness.

"What cat?" he said.

"That DAMNED cat!" Clancy's calm shattered. "That cat
that's been spying on us for weeks, that nasty thing that tried to
kill me after our first service, what other cat *could* it be, Hertz!
That stinking cat snuck into the Reverend's car and rode home
with him and now he's going to stay there!"

"How do you know?!" said the worm reasonably.

"He was talking about it on the PHONE!" Clancy drew out

this final word in a moan, and Hertz' patience with histrionics, never long, became strained.

"Calm down!" he said. "I told you, it's not the end of the world. So what? Good for him. At least that cat won't be stalking around here anymore. You should be happy. What's the problem?"

Hertz knew instantly he should have known better than to make light. He had seen the rodent lose control before, with the result that he, Hertz, was baptized in a toilet after breaking his promise to the rat to accept Jesus Christ as his personal Lord and Savior. But this time the rat was not just angry, he was also hurt. He clenched his paws as tight as he could and shrieked with the self-inflicted pain. "It's not fair!" he cried. "That cat isn't a Christian! *I* should be the Reverend's friend, and go home with him at night, and not have to stay here hidden away in that stinky basement! *I'm* the one that started a church for all of us who get left out. *I'm* the one that God chose! And I don't get any thanks at all for anything, because I'm nothing but a dirty stinking rat with orange teeth! Oh God, why are you so mean to me!" And then, like Samson, possessed with that blind and demonic strength that follows upon betrayal, he rammed himself headlong up against the plastic casing of the unsteady and top-heavy composter, and knocked it over on its side, spilling its dark and rich and rotting and worm-eaten guts onto the dry ground. Hertz didn't know what had hit him, when he found himself, along with his countless descendants, wriggling frantically under the bright hot and deadly noonday sunshine.

❧

HARDLY AWARE OF what he'd done or what he was doing, Clancy took off into the woods. It was Steven, who, having witnessed the whole catastrophe from his favorite perch, leaped into action. He'd been resting on the roof's edge, just above the scene of destruction, and heard it all.

Even steady Steven was overwhelmed by the degree of chaos. Compost was spilled out across the concrete walkway between the church building and the community garden, and there were writhing worms everywhere. What could one pigeon do? There was no way he could lift up and put the composter back on its feet, much less fill it back up with its inhabitants! But unless someone did something, countless worms would die. Steven considered for a moment, and then took wing.

☙❧

GRACE HAD HER HEADPHONES ON, listening to an audiobook while she went over the various items in the weekly parish newsletter and maneuvered them around like jigsaw puzzle pieces in her outdated Microsoft Publisher template. It was her least favorite regular task and always took her longer than she had time for. This is why, she always said, the secretary needs a secretary. And so it was a good while before she became aware of the tapping at the window to the right of her desk.

☙❧

STEVEN KNEW that if any creature could put the composter back to rights, it was the kind that put it there in the first place. So it was Grace he thought of immediately. But no matter how hard he tapped, she didn't seem to hear him! He even cooed at the top of his voice, but of course that wasn't any more effective. At one point she did glance over, but then turned right back to her screen. It was frustrating. He pecked and tapped and his beak became not a little sore at the base. But the human glaring at the screen on her desk was his only hope.

It is the case that all things come to an end, and that includes audiobooks and the layout of church bulletins. After what felt to Steven like an eternity, Grace leaned back in her chair, removed her reading glasses, rubbed her eyes, and removed her headphones. Steven, seeing his chance, tapped with all his strength. After a moment, she looked over at him. And looked away again. Steven's heart sank, but he did not falter. He tapped and tapped, and it occurred to him to break up the rhythm a bit. That might make her pay attention.

It did. The woman at the desk looked over at the window, scowled quizzically and cocked her head in a curious, questioning gesture, not unlike what a bird might do. Steven knew that the battle wasn't yet won. He kept on tapping, changing up the rhythm, but at a very fast pace, for countless lives depended upon him.

Grace Holbach was at once annoyed and fascinated. For Pete's sake, if it wasn't bad enough that she had a million things to do before the end of the week, now a crazy bird had come along to make everything all the more difficult by making such a racket. My God, you'd think the crazy thing was trying to break in! All they needed was a bird loose in the church, pooping all over the place. And of course everyone knows that it's bad luck to let a bird get in the house. She figured that was all the more true of a church.

She sighed, stood, and went over to the window. "Shoo!" she said, and drummed her fingernails against the pane of glass. "Get." And she wiggled her fingers at the creature. Now that she was up close she could see that it was a pigeon. Filthy birds.

But the pigeon did not flinch; it just kept right on tapping. Grace then regarded it with a burgeoning uneasiness. My God, she'd never known a pigeon, or any other bird that was not a trained pet, to stay put when a human being got this close, even through a barrier. She furrowed her brow, put her hands on her hips, and bent her knees, until she was roughly eye level with the crazy thing. And it continued to tap away. She blinked several times, as someone would who is coming back to consciousness after a faint.

She spoke out loud to herself. "I'm damned if this pigeon isn't trying to get my attention!" She held up her right index finger, as one would who is trying to silently indicate that they will be right back. She crossed the room to the firmly closed door to the Reverend's office, and just as firmly knocked.

"Silas," she called. "Get out here a second."

"What is it, Grace...I'm..."

"Just come out here...it's important." She was led back over to the window, where Steven continued to tap away, strengthened and encouraged by his success in getting her attention.

Soon the woman was joined by a man in a tabbed white collar. "Look at that," she said. "Watch." And once again she bent her knees to be eye level with the bird, and placed her fingers against the glass, right at the point at which Steven's bill touched the window. The bird kept tapping. "See!" she cried. "Can you believe it? This pigeon has been tapping on my window for I don't know how long! I had my headphones on. Obviously, he's trying to get my attention! You think something's wrong with it? Should I call animal control?"

The priest was silent for such a long moment that Grace wrested her gaze from the window to regard her employer.

She was surprised by what she saw. The young priest's dark eyes had a faraway expression, and the corners of his mouth quivered. "Silas?" she said, rather uneasy.

The priest put his fingertips lightly to his chin. "Birds are smarter than you think," he said. "I'm going outside."

◦※◦

SHE FOLLOWED him out the main entrance to the church, outside the chapel, and they went round the left cornerstone and down the side of the building to the windowsill where the pigeon perched, as if waiting. As the two humans approached, the woman behind the man, down the narrow stretch of ground between the church and the old chain link fence that marked the property line, Steven held his place until the man was right next to him. Then Steven leaped and landed on top of the chain link fencepost a few yards ahead. Steven flew to the edge of the lid of the rain barrel at the corner of the building, underneath the raised gutter spout, and waited until the two humans reached that corner. Then he flew to the upturned bottom edge of the overturned composter and spread his wings several times and emitted a long low cooing vocalization.

"Silas!" Grace cried. "I'll be damned! Someone's knocked over the composter!"

That, of course, was obvious. The composter lay on its side like a felled tree, having spilled a fetid quantity of rotting vegetable matter alive with the wriggling of countless worms who were still writhing in aimless panic, their world having lost its reliable foundation.

The priest retched a little as the stench of the stuff reached him. "God!" he gagged. "What a mess!" He looked around and stepped back and looked up at Steven, who had flown to the edge of the roof just above, and the pigeon seemed to be looking right back at the priest, undaunted and intelligent, and the priest seemed to take a cue from this. He took a deep breath...and then looked down at the squirming mess. "Grace, we have do something."

Grace had already set the composter back on its legs. She then squatted, bracing her hands on her thighs, and peered all around and inside the composter for any clue as to what might have made it fall. It seemed perfectly intact. And it was right where she'd placed it after the last frost was over. She supposed it was possible that a strong wind could have knocked it down, but there was barely a breeze. "Must have been some kid," she said. "I'd like to get my hands on him." She stood up, hands on hips. She regarded the hundreds of worms writhing in the filth on the ground with distaste. Then she shrieked as the priest bent and gathered up a quantity of them in his bare cupped hands.

"Silas! What the hell are you doing!?"

"We've got to save them, Grace! I mean, we have to get these worms back in there. Or they'll die. Don't you see! That's why the pigeon came to the window! He came to get us to help! If he hadn't..." Reverend De Bassompierre dumped his handful of worms into the lowest tray of the composter, where they landed with a squelch. He bent to scoop up another load. Grace watched, wide-eyed.

"Silas! Your hands! For God's sake! Let me go get the shovel! It's in the utility closet!"

The priest turned on his secretary as if she'd blasphemed. "NO! You'll hurt them!"

"Them?! The worms?! What's gotten into you!?"

The priest dropped his second load of worms rather clumsily on top of the first, and turned to Grace with one filthy hand dripping compost juice onto his shoe, and the other lifted up to point to Steven, who now was perched on the edge of the roof of the church.

"HE CAME TO US FOR HELP!" The young priest's voice rose like a missile, and his eyes were wide and shining with unshed tears.

Grace, who was a mother of a teenaged boy, knew when she was not going to get anywhere by using common sense. Her boss was, at least for the time being, and for whatever reason, having a moment. "All right," she said, and she took off her rings and rolled up her sleeves to help.

❧

HERTZ WAS HORRIFIED by the close presence of the two human beings, even as he was scooped—with unnecessary roughness, he felt—along with dozens of his descendants back into the dark safety of the righted composter. Even when the last little worm had been restored to the container, there was absolute bedlam, for every tunnel and every chamber in every level of the compost bin—all the work that had gone into organizing the chaos of rotting vegetable matter over the passing days!—was completely undone. Hertz was forced into a role for which he was particularly unsuited, that of an encourager. He had to take the lead, however, otherwise nothing would get done. For the next few hours he was obliged to make his way through the destruction and give support and direction to all of his offspring. By the time he was finished, he had never been so exhausted in his life. He dug himself a makeshift chamber near the top of the heap and coiled himself tight and swore that to his dying breath he would never again allow that blasted rat anywhere near his colony ever again. He would put his metaphorical foot down and he knew it wasn't going to be pretty. But if the rat couldn't hold himself together—and obviously, he couldn't—he was going to have to keep his distance. It was a matter of public safety.

❧❧❧

STEVEN WAS STILL on the roof above the now righted composter when Ottoline returned from her visit to their daughter. "Hello, dear," she said. "How was your day?"

"Bad news," he said. "The Reverend flipped."

"What?!"

Steven related, in so many words, that the Reverend emerged from the cellar, had a heated discussion with the big worm, lost his temper, knocked over the composter, then took off into the woods. Steven then told her that he hadn't known what else to do but get the attention of one of the humans, so he'd tapped on Grace's window and brought them out, and they had put the composter back on its feet.

"Steven!" Ottoline was aghast. "You didn't! My word!"

Steven nodded.

"Well!" Ottoline looked at her husband with an amalgamation of wonder and unease. Never before had she known of anyone to purposefully attract the attention of a human being, so capricious and potentially dangerous and unreasonable even the best of those beings were understood by all to be. It was an act so unfathomable that it transcended taboo—it was simply not done. And here Stephen had done it...for the sake of the worms. "Steven," she said. "You are something else."

Steven was looking towards the woods. "Reverend's gone, though."

"He'll be back," she said. "He can't survive in the woods."

As soon as the words left her beak, she knew that they were terribly true, truer than she intended. "Oh Steven!" she said. "We have to find him!"

※

THERE WAS ONLY ONE HOPE—OR two, as they figured. Ottoline and Steven agreed that the best nostrils for the daunting and possibly dangerous task of ferreting an apparently unhinged Reverend rodent out of the woods belonged to the two scavenger birds...Bertram and/or Donna.

"I'll go talk to Donna," said Ottoline. I know she'll help. I just hope..." She filled her prominent pigeon's breast with air, then released it in an anxious coo. "I just hope there won't be any trouble. Do you think Bertram will be willing to help? After what happened..."

Steven did not answer. Ottoline knew what he was thinking regardless.

"You're right," she replied, even though Steven hadn't sung a note. "This is an emergency, and surely Bertram can overcome his hurt feelings to help save the Reverend from himself. And if he can't ... but of course, we have to do him the justice of asking. Steven...be careful."

Steven took off without a word.

※

"OF COURSE, OTTOLINE," the magnificent, dazzling vulture said. "Of course."

"Oh, Donna. Thank heavens. We just don't know where else
to turn. Steven is going to try to talk to Bertram, but... Well, you
know how he might react. We have to try, though. You do think
you might be able to sniff him out? He wouldn't have to be.. ?"
She couldn't finish the thought.

Donna the vulture spoke with quiet confidence. "Not at all.
After all, Ottoline, life isn't just about finding the next meal. I
can sniff out anything, living or dead, when I have to. I think I
can easily smell a rat. Especially in the woods, where so many of
them fear to tread. Don't worry. Between myself and
Bertram...and I do think Bertram *will* help...we'll bring the
Reverend home safe and sound." And so saying, she spread her
enormous wings and took off in a flying leap towards the dense
darkness of the Croatan National Forest, leaving Ottoline to
admire her strange elegance.

༺❧༻

BERTRAM WAS BROODING, perched on the very topmost branch
of a long dead pine near his family roost. He felt exceptionally
ill-tempered this day. The pickings had been slim along the
interstate, and his sisters had complained about the toughness
of the five-day-old rattlesnake corpse he'd brought home for
lunch, even though he'd tenderized it as best he could with his
own gastric acid. There was just no pleasing his family
sometimes.

He was supposed to be back on the scavenge for supper, but
he was in no hurry to be insulted again. He sat on the branch
and consoled himself with the notion that he cut a sinister figure
as he glowered over the landscape. In the distance he could just
make out the strictly ornamental empty belfry of St. Aloysius,
atop the cross of which he knew Ottoline sometimes enjoyed
perching. With his sharp eyes he could see that no one was
perched there now; no doubt Ottoline was on some errand for
the Reverend. She always did anything that dirty rat asked. It

was pathetic. To think that he, Bertram, had ever trusted that
...rat.

Bertram saw red, as he always did whenever he thought
about what had happened with Donna. His outlook, in fact, was
at that moment so colored by bitterness that he did not see, nor
hear, nor even smell, nor in any way detect the swift approach of
Steven.

"Son," Steven began, saying a great deal in that one word.
"We need your help."

At first Bertram's heart, as if independent of the rest of him,
leaped in his breast, because it was glad to see the pigeon. But
soon enough his defenses rose. His claws tightened around the
dead branch that was his perch. "Go away."

Steven had landed on a branch just below the buzzard. He
looked up at him and did not budge.

Bertram spread his wings, though whether to take off or to
try to intimidate his visitor, it wasn't really clear. But he neither
took off, nor was Steven intimidated. Bertram folded in his wings
and looked down at the pigeon. "What kind of help?' he grumbled, making sure not to sound as if he cared.

"The Reverend's in trouble," the pigeon said. "Lost in the
woods. Hasn't been himself since the wedding, and this morning
he lost his temper and just about killed all the worms. He didn't
mean to, but he's real upset. We've got to find him and bring him
on home. And quick. He can't be out there on his own for long
like the rest of us. He don't know how to protect himself. We
need your nose, son."

At the mere mention of the 'Reverend,' Bertram's claws had
tightened even more, and Steven could feel the tension even in
the wood of the branch upon which he was perched. But he said
his piece and remained looking up at the buzzard, steadfast and
silent.

Bertram heard his daddy's voice in his own head. "It's a trick.
They're up to something."

He spat. "Why don't you just ask his precious Donna to look for him?"

Steven hopped up to the topmost branch and perched beside the bitter buzzard. "Ottoline's asking her. She'll help. But it's a big forest, and we don't have much time. Come on, son. You don't want nothing to happen to the Reverend."

Bertram had a sudden burst of memory, as if a stone had been dropped into the pool of his mind. He saw himself, as if from the outside, descending to the edge of the boulevard, where the then unknown Clancy stood guard over the corpse of a freshly flattened squirrel. He remembered it all, in waves—that first encounter, the first service he attended, his baptism, his introduction of Donna. He saw himself in these waves of memory as if he were no longer himself. It was like seeing a familiar stranger. He had the sensation of stretching out his neck and beak to grasp something that was, at the point of contact, no longer there. He suddenly felt inexpressibly sad. And he saw the Reverend in these memories and knew, somehow, that if the Reverend disappeared, as bad as he now felt, he would feel much much worse. For he realized he had never been as happy as when he had been a member of the church.

But did he want to be happy, when he could not be happy with Donna? That, he knew, was the question, and there was no answer. To be happy without her meant that he would have to let her be on her own, and he did not want to.

Steven could feel the buzzard's talons relax around the branch they shared. The pigeon took off, and the buzzard followed.

❧❦❧

NOT FAR INTO THE WOODS, but much further in than he'd ever been before, Clancy's instinct was to bury himself, and so he did, but he found that he couldn't stay covered up for long without becoming dizzy. Every few minutes he had to poke his snout out of the dirt for air, and after a while even that wasn't enough to ward off lightheadedness. And the dampness of the earth was making him feel uncomfortably clammy. He was hidden, but he was not safe. He wasn't meant to survive underground. He wasn't an earthworm, after all.

This thought, of course, caused a wave of fresh anguish to overcome him, and he cried out. He would never forgive himself for what he'd done. Life as he knew it was over, and as if to prove it, he dug himself deeper into the ground. But still he couldn't stop himself from coming up for air. Eventually he wearied of constantly having to rise, so he unearthed himself and climbed a little ways up the trunk of the nearest tree, and hid as best he could in the crook of a branch.

❧

OTTOLINE AND STEVEN decided that Ottoline should remain at the church, in the unlikely event the Reverend might find his way back of his own accord. Steven would accompany Bertram on his search of the western portion of the woods, and Donna would cover the east. In very little time, Ottoline was witness to the curious and unusual sight of the two great scavenger birds, mirror images of one another in the sky, circling high above their respective sectors of the forest.

It had not escaped the notice or the concern of the rest of the members of the St. Aloysius Jr. community that the Reverend had toppled the composter and run off. When they saw Ottoline perched as a sentry on top of the restored structure, they gathered around.

"What's going on?" chittered Timmy the dead squirrel's father. "We heard the Reverend damn near killed all the worms! What's his problem, Ottoline?"

Before Ottoline could answer, a raccoon piped up. "I saw the whole thing," she tsked. "It was crazy. I think he must have rabies."

"That is unhelpful and ridiculous speculation," Ottoline remonstrated. "I don't want to hear any more gossip like that. Rats do not get rabies, anyway. You all know as well as I do that the Reverend has been under a great deal of strain lately, and I'm afraid it's simply gotten the better of him. At the moment he needs our prayers and support, not our harsh and ill-informed judgments."

"Well you don't have to get huffy," said the raccoon. "I was only trying to help. Where has he run off to, anyway?"

"If we knew that, there wouldn't be any problem," said Ottoline. "All we know is that he took off into the woods, and since he has absolutely no familiarity with that territory, we have to assume he's lost and in danger. Steven and I have asked Donna and Bertram to do their best to sniff him out...so I'm sure it won't be long until they find him, but in the meantime, it's very concerning."

"Donna *and* Bertram?" exclaimed the mother opossum. "*That's* a switch! I heard that Bertram caught her and the—"

Ottoline's breast grew so indignantly full that she had to raise her beak. "For heaven's sake, this gossip has no place in a Christian community! Now, as for Bertram and the Reverend, there is nothing between them more substantial than a misunderstanding, and in times of crisis, reasonable individuals—especially those who are church members committed to following the example of Jesus Christ—are able and willing to put any and all differences aside in order to respond. I hope that all of us would do the same and work together. Think, for a moment, how you would feel if you had caused damage to the property of someone for whom you care deeply. Think how you would feel if you had —without intending to, but in the heat of emotion—put an entire group in danger! Think about it! We all know that the Reverend is the gentlest of souls, and that he would never want to cause even the slightest trouble to anyone. But he is only rodent, and there's only so much pressure that any of us can handle. The Reverend expects too much of himself, and we have ourselves to blame in part for that. Now is the time for all of us to come together to support him...if it isn't too late."

Hearing this last through one of the ventilation holes in the side of the composter, Hertz squirmed.

Timmy the dead squirrel's father, for one, felt chastened and galvanized by Ottoline's remonstration. "I'll help look for the Reverend," he said. "I don't have a nose like those vultures, but I know these woods pretty well, you know."

"Thank you, dear," said Ottoline. "That's the spirit!"

"I'll look, too," said a buck deer by the name of Magnus, who had attended the past few services, though standing at a distance. "I like your Reverend. He's high strung, but I'm used to that. And I'm good at being able to tell if something's out of the ordinary in the woods."

Ottoline regarded the deer with real appreciation. "Thank you so much. I imagine with your height you'll have a unique perspective that may just prove crucial."

"Well, there's that, too," said Magnus. "I'll get started..." And he bounded into the woods as quick as he could. He never liked to linger for long out in the open.

With that a silence descended over what remained of the gathering. Ottoline waited.

"We'll go help," said the mother opossum, her six young fry clinging to her fur. "Fourteen more eyes out looking can't hurt."

"Very true," said Ottoline. "But be careful."

She was heartened by the congregation's reluctant, yet sincere spirit of altruism. "Be sure to look out for one another. I'll be here, just in case. Please be careful." She wished the Reverend could know how concern for him had brought the congregation together like never before. "It will all work out," she said to herself. "It must."

Just below her, Hertz could not believe his rudimentary ears. He withdrew and curled into himself. He felt ill. After all the trouble the rodent had caused his colony, it served him right to get lost, but now it sounded like the silly rat might not make it back. Far be it from Hertz to pray, but he did mutter a little demand, to whatever capricious force might order and/or maintain the universe, that the rodent should live to face his, Hertz's wrath, and no other's.

❧❦❧

TURNING and turning in the widening gyre ...Bertram circled the woods, taking in a spectrum of odors with every breath. Living wood, dead wood, pine sap, mulch, the urine and excrement of various creatures, and undergirding it all the rich dense smell of earth. But there wasn't even the slightest hint of that distinctive, rather corn-like odor of the rat. And yet Bertram felt quite strongly that Clancy was down there somewhere, more alive than dead.

In the distance he could see Donna circling her own portion of the forest. He couldn't stop his imagination from conjuring up images of heroism and vindication. He would catch the scent of the Reverend and descend, discover him, and then what? Finding the lost Reverend alive, what would he do? He had imagined so many times, over the past weeks, a confrontation, in which he, Bertram, would expose the rat, in the presence of the entire congregation, for what he was, a sneaky, selfish charlatan. And he, Bertram, would then leave them all to their shattered delusions and return to noble solitude.

Now the Reverend had disgraced himself, and Bertram's fantasy of revenge fell limp as a worm within his imagination. Once again Bertram caught a glimpse of Donna across the sky. Something about the vision of her, alone and at a distance, revealed to him her particular incomprehensible individuality, an utterly distinct being from himself. She was alone, he was alone, the Reverend was alone, and the scene on the water tower he now recognized for what it was—his own refusal to face the truth, and his own terrible need to possess another creature completely, and to dominate. He was just like his daddy, hellbent on having what he wanted, his way and no other. He could see now that the Reverend had been scared to death, and had run to Donna for protection and not out of desire. And Bertram's bitterness in an instant transferred itself from the Reverend to his own daddy, who'd planted suspicion deeper within his soul than he'd ever realized.

❦

IT WAS Bertram who caught the scent, but as it happened, it was patient Steven who made the first contact. Bertram, who had begun to wonder, after hours of swooping and circling on an empty stomach, if he might need to take a break, was descending to snack on the remains of a pitifully small snake he'd come across olfactorily, when another smell, faint but familiar, caught his notice, mulchy and sharp with angst and with an underscent like a cornfield in the rain. It was like...It could be...it was...the Reverend. Bertram trained his sharp eye on a spot, not far from the edge of the woods after all, but far enough in so that a small creature like the Reverend would certainly lose his bearings...He began to spiral down.

Huzzah! He thought as he descended. He had done it! *He* sniffed out the Reverend...and *he* was going to save the day! He could see it all in his mind's eye as if it were already a treasured memory, returning to the churchyard in triumph with the rat...eternally grateful...astride his long neck. Ottoline would be overjoyed, the rest of the congregation would be elated, and Donna! Well, Donna would be pleased. Bertram would like to think that she would be impressed, and that she would as a result find him irresistible...but here even fantasy could not strain without breaking. Donna, he knew, would know better than anybody that it was nothing but luck that he'd caught the scent before she did, that the lost Reverend happened to have been lost within his sector of the woods rather than hers. She would simply be glad the search was over.

Nothing would really change the way she felt about him or herself.

Bertram could see as well as smell the Reverend now. The rodent was curled up into himself, eyes wide, the end of his tail in his mouth, and secreted, insofar as his size would allow, into the crook of a thick low branch spreading from a mature maple tree, about four feet from the forest floor. Bertram spread his wings wide to slow his descent, and was about to call the Reverend's name, but before he could speak the rat bolted upright, stiffened, shrieked, and leaped from the maple tree and took off deeper into the woods. Bertram started after him, but it was no use. The rodent wouldn't stop running. Bertram took off toward the church, to let Ottoline know that at least the Reverend was still alive.

SUFFERING FROM EXPOSURE, freezing, and half delirious with sleeplessness, discomfort and sheer stress, Clancy had not recognized, in the dark descending spreading shape, his former friend and parishioner Bertram. He'd seen only the looming, overshadowing form of a bird of prey coming to devour him. Completely beside himself, unaware, in that moment, of where or who or even what he was, his only impulse was to escape. And so he kept running aimlessly until, overcome by exhaustion, he stumbled up against the root of an oak. He climbed up the trunk as high as he could and clung there, like one of the infant opossums to its mother's side.

BEFORE BERTRAM REACHED the churchyard he came upon Steven. "I found him," the buzzard said, "but he ran off." And he told the pigeon what had happened.

"Find him again. You can do it. And when you do, just don't

get too close. I'll wait here. Just come get me. I'll be on the roof."

"Okay," said Bertram, grateful for this advice that came without the upbraiding he was accustomed to. He wished his daddy could be more like Steven.

❦

BERTRAM RETURNED, having pretty easily picked up the Reverend's scent, not far from where he'd lost it before. Steven had given the matter thought, and had decided upon a plan. "The whole church is out there looking now, Ottoline says. Find everyone, and tell them to come here to me. We'll take care of this together. We'll set up a perimeter, so if he gets spooked, he won't get any farther in the woods."

Bertram looked to the west, to the familiar figure circling over the dark treetops. He looked back at Steven, and he didn't have to ask. With a deep odiferous sigh, he took off to tell Donna first.

❦

BERTRAM LED the way into the woods; Steven was close behind him, and the congregation followed, with Donna bringing up the rear along with the mother opossum, heavily but seemingly contentedly burdened by her six little children. Donna had indeed been pleased that Bertram had been the one to find the Reverend, and when he'd approached her in the air to let her know, she was touched by the change in him. "Donna," he'd gurgled quietly, in a measured, deliberately formal tone. "I found him. The Reverend. He's on a tree, not too far in the woods after all. He's upset, though, and Steven thinks we should all go together to bring him home. He says to meet at the composter."

"All right," she said. "Thank you, Bertram, for telling me."

She wondered if she perhaps should not have said his name,

for, hearing it, he'd grunted and took off without another word. She'd flown at a respectful distance behind him to the composter to be joined by the rest of the searchers, and then Steven led the way back into the woods. Donna trundled in alongside the opossum, and to distract herself from the tension with Bertram she struck up a conversation. "This certainly has been an eventful evening," she said.

"Sure has," said the opossum agreeably. "Can't get over it. Seemed like such a nice fellow; too bad he had to go crazy like that. I still think it could be rabies, like the raccoon said. Glad I don't have to worry about getting that mess."

"Oh, I don't think the Reverend has rabies," said Donna. "I just think he's under too much pressure and doesn't know how to ask for help."

"You sound like Ottoline," said the opossum. "Well, maybe ya'll are right. But I know one thing: if I was one of them worms in that composter, I wouldn't be in such a hurry for that rat to climb on top of my bin and preach too soon."

Donna murmured that she hoped that the worms weren't too traumatized. She thought it might be good to change the subject. "Your young ones are so well-behaved!" she said. "Still, it must take a lot out of you to carry them all around like that."

"They know they better hang on tight!" said their mother jauntily. "You got kids, hon?"

"Yes...two...they're with their father..." And at that point, to Donna's relief, the procession came to a pause, and Steven flew up onto a low branch to address them.

"We're coming up on the Reverend...He's just ahead. Now listen. We'll spread out, and make a circle around him, and in case he gets spooked and runs away, we'll have a better chance of heading him off."

"Right smart, ain't he? The pigeon?" remarked the mother opossum. "Who would've thunk, as pea tiny as his head is. Maybe *he* ought to be Reverend now."

Donna disagreed, but didn't want to argue. "He does have an air of authority, doesn't he?" she said.

⚜

STEVEN DIDN'T HAVE to draw close to see that the rodent was in an altered state, unnaturally stiff, as if he were nothing more than a grotesque outgrowth of the trunk he was clinging to. Steven approached on the ground, in a series of hops, until he was about a yard away from the tree. "Reverend," he cooed. "Come on back to church. It's not safe for you out here."

No answer. The rodent just clung to the tree. Steven waited. After a long silence, in which the ominous and pagan call of an owl could be heard, he spoke again.

"Reverend. The whole church is here, everybody's been looking for you, 'cept Ottoline, she stayed behind in case you got back on your own. Bertram found you; he and Donna sniffed the whole woods out to get a whiff of you, and he came and got me 'cause he figured you might be afraid he's still upset with you. No one's upset with you, Reverend. We just want you to be back home with us and preach to us again."

No response. The rat did not even blink. Steven waited and waited, and while he waited he noticed that the tail of the rat was raw and scabbed near the end from having been gnawed to a pulp. Only then did it occur to the pigeon that there was only one way to break the spell of fear and shame that had the Reverend in a death grip. "I'll be right back," he said, and flew through the trees back to Donna. "Quick!" he said. "Go get that worm."

⚜

OTTOLINE WAS ALARMED when she saw Donna flying in from the woods by herself, and flew down from the ornamental belfry to meet her by the composter. "What's going on?" said the pigeon. "Is the Reverend all right?"

Donna wasn't sure how to answer that without worrying her friend. "He's unharmed," she ventured. "But very upset. Steven asked me to come get 'the worm.'"

Ottoline blinked. The worm, she knew, could only mean Hertz, a difficult character, far from the most compassionate or cooperative creature in the world, and more likely than not feeling ill-disposed toward the Reverend. Not without justification. "Oh my," she said. She regarded the composter as one might regard a hornet's nest. "He means Hertz, the Reverend's oldest friend."

❧

"WELL..." said Ottoline rather nervously. "Steven knows best, I suppose." She trotted over with a somewhat apprehensive air, and tapped with her beak upon the composter casing. "Beg pardon," she began. "Mr. Hertz...this is Ottoline. We do need your help, I'm afraid. I'm sorry to disturb you, after all that's happened, but this is urgent."

❧

IT TOOK SOME PERSUASION, but not too much. Ottoline, once the grizzled worm could be cajoled into extending his tip through one of the ventilation holes of the composter, explained to him that the Reverend had been located, but that he was in a very precarious psychological state, and that he needed the encouragement and support of all of his friends. Hertz told Ottoline that the rat was always in a precarious psychological state, and that what he really needed was to get a grip before he killed somebody.

"Be that as it may," said Ottoline. "This is no time for reproaches. The Reverend is in danger. "

It was Donna, however, who convinced the worm to help. "He just needs to see that you're alive," she said. "And then to come back here where he's safe. Then you can give him hell."

Hertz regarded Donna with grudging respect. He found her, as he found all birds, repulsive and sinister. But she was no dummy. "All right," he said. "Let's get this over with."

☙❧

AGAIN OTTOLINE STAYED BEHIND. She felt strongly that it would be best if at least she, his right paw, did not see the Reverend at his weakest. She watched as the vulture, with the worm dangling from her beak, circled and then disappeared into the woods, a phantasmagoric, yet heartening sight.

☙❧

MEANWHILE, the other congregants of St. Aloysius Jr., having formed a ring around the area containing the tree to which their reverend clung, waited and watched. Donna, with Hertz on board, flew directly to Steven, and placed the worm beside him.

"Here you are," said Steven. "Let's go." And he opened his beak and reached for the worm's midsection.

"Wait a minute!" Hertz said with a good deal of heat. "Close that trap. I'm sick and tired of being mouthed in half. Get me that deer. And with a thrust of his tip, he indicated that noble mammal just to their right.

Steven hesitated. The deer was a gentle soul, but so big, and relatively new to the community. Wouldn't he be sure to spook the Reverend into another blind dash? But he wasn't going to argue with the worm. He darted over to the deer, who nodded and came over.

"That's better," said Hertz, and the deer lowered his head and Hertz wrapped himself around the topmost tip of the left antler. "Perfect. Forward march," he said.

And the deer and the worm approached that tree.

෧෯෯

MAGNUS MOVED SLOWLY and almost completely without noise, then came to a full stop and lowered himself to his haunches. He lifted his head so that his rack of antlers came very near the rat, though still not within touching distance. The deer cast his eyes down, as if he were humbling himself before a potentate.

The worm and the rat were level with one another, about a foot apart. "Hey," said the worm, not without a note of caution. "It's me. Still alive and wiggling, as you can see. A little shook up, but it takes more than a tantrum to get rid of me, as you well know!"

The spellbound rodent did not move a muscle. If he heard the worm's voice, or saw him, there was no indication. But the worm was undaunted. "Listen," he said. "No one got hurt, but that was a real mess you made, and it COULD have been lights out for me. What got into you? You know I don't believe in devils and demons or any of that crap, but for Ground's sake, it isn't like you to get homicidal! So *what* if that silly human's got that cat in his house! And by the way, you may be interested in knowing, that if it weren't for that Reverend DeBassoon, and Grace, too, I'd be dead meat. Lucky for you—and me—those good-for-nothings were good for something for once... I don't know how they got wind, but it wasn't but a few minutes after you knocked us over before they came out and scooped us all back into the composter. We're all alive, but of course getting everything back the way it was—the way it was supposed to be in there before you turned it all upside down—might kill us yet! Anyway, what's done is done, and running away isn't gonna get you off the hook with me. You owe me one now, big time. Get yourself together and come on back to the church. I've got work to do and so do you."

Clancy didn't stir. His eyes continued to stare blankly, his whiskers held their terrified and mortified stiffness, his tail drooped lifelessly and seeped blood and pus from where he'd gnawed it raw. There was no indication that he heard a word the worm had said. But the mention of the word *church* set off a slow, heavy burst of sickening pain deep in his abdomen, exactly as if some sinister and invisible hand had gripped, twisted and squeezed his prominent testicles. He did not realize that he himself was pressing them flat up against the tough bark of the tree. A deep moan escaped him, like the final note of funeral hymn. "I hate myself," he seemed to the worm to say.

"Join the club," said the worm drily. "Now hop on and let's get back to where we belong. It stinks out here."

❦

OTTOLINE THOUGHT she must be dreaming, when through the milky film of her transparent eyelids she saw, emerging from the woods in the pale uncanny light of the moon and stars, a most extraordinary procession of variegated wildlife species, familiar but strange in the half-light, at the head of which was the buck deer, upon whose left antler clung, with all four paws and a prehensile tail, a shivering rat. Behind this strode the congregational search party, including Bertram and Donna, with Steven at the rear, for all the world as if they were lost sheep who had searched for and found their lost shepherd.

❦

AND SO THE congregation of St Aloysius Jr. returned, in nocturnal triumph, to their church in the open air, and Ottoline leaped from the cross atop the ornamental belfry to meet them on the ground. "Oh, thank heavens," was all she could say. She watched as the deer, upon approaching the composter, bent his legs and bowed his head, and the Reverend, shivering and bedraggled and miserable-looking but alive, relaxed his hold and dropped a foot or so onto the ground with a tired thud. The rat then reached up for the worm, who allowed himself to be unwound and carried yokelike across the rat's back to the composter, into which he disappeared instantly. Then the Reverend Clancy looked around as if he was just waking up from a dream.

The deer stood up; wordlessly, but with an air of excusing himself, he turned and loped off into the woods. Ottoline noted the beginnings of a pale glimmer of light rising on the eastern horizon. "Well," she said. "It has been a very long night. I think we should all get some rest now." She glanced at the Reverend, who was on all fours, hunched into himself, but no longer shivering. Everyone was looking at him, and he knew it.

Ottoline began to approach him, but Steven, behind Clancy, caught her eye, and she stopped short. "Good night, everyone," she said to those who remained. She could not resist adding, with an anxious glance at the Reverend, "See you all on Sunday."

The Reverend, if he heard, did not react. Ottoline and Steven lifted themselves on the air to the edge of the roof of the church, and then took off.

And then, one by one, with varying degrees of reluctance, the animals departed until only the rat remained before the composter, still and prostrate, like a petitioner before a potentate. After a while he reached for his tail, and stood and put his snout to the ventilation holes on the side of the composter.

"Hertz," he said in a tone so devoid of his usual intensity of excitement or distress that he scarcely sounded like himself. He waited a long time for the response that reluctantly came. "What do you want now?!" cried the worm.

Clancy did not know what he wanted from the worm, the friend whose life and livelihood and legacy he had so insensibly endangered. He only knew that he could not just creep into the cellar and wrap himself up in the choir robes and go to sleep as if nothing had happened. He could not wake up later in the day and prepare a sermon for Sunday. He could not call himself a

Reverend, or even a Christian, after being so bad, until he knew one thing. "Hertz, can you ever forgive me?"

"FOR GROUND'S SAKE, JUST DON'T DO ANYTHING LIKE THAT EVER AGAIN! NOW LEAVE ME ALONE AND LET ME GET SOME SLEEP!"

And Clancy accepted this penance. He walked away, squeezed himself through the crawlspace door and across the cellar and up the stairs and down the hall to the sanctuary, and tried to forgive himself.

HOLY COMMUNION

"Is that Ottoline? Or is it Steven? I know it must be one of them, I can tell by the tail. See how it's pointy at the tip— and how mine fans out? But upside down like that, I can't tell which one of them it's supposed to be."

Clancy didn't know what Bertram was talking about. He was showing his restored parishioner around the outside of the church building, but Clancy had not pointed out, because he had never paid much attention to, the small round stained-glass window that was set into the brickwork up above them, where the vaulted south wall of the chapel neared its apex. It was a simple, rather abstract depiction of the Holy Spirit in the form of a dove, descending headlong towards a goblet shape in which crimson-colored glass represented the Blood of Christ. Attached to the protrusion of the Spirit's beak was a small white disc clearly meant to represent a Eucharistic wafer. Regarding it now, Clancy did suppose that in its overall shape the Spirit did somewhat resemble Ottoline and Steve, though of course they never descended headlong like that, but flapped and fluttered when they landed, and certainly they never flew with their beaks full.

"Oh Lord!" cried Clancy. "No, no, that's not Ottoline or Steven. That's the Holy Spirit! Of course you couldn't have

known, but in the Bible the Holy Spirit looks like a dove sometimes. Ottoline and Steven are pigeons, not doves...I don't
believe I've ever *seen* a dove, come to think of it! Maybe they all
live in the Holy Land..."

"Oh." Bertram felt mild disappointment. He'd begun to
wonder—if Ottoline or Steven could be featured in a window,
perhaps he could be too! But it sounded like these pictures in
the windows of the church were of creatures in the Bible, not in
the world.

"Are there any buzzards in the Bible?" he asked his pastor.

Clancy had to admit that he did not know. The two creatures
continued to gaze at the image in the window.

"What's it doing?" Bertram said after a moment.

"Well, you see that thing in his beak? That's the body of our
Lord and Savior Jesus Christ, who is the bread of life. And the
red stuff in that cup? That's His blood. When Reverend DeBassompierre asks the Holy Spirit to change some bread and some
wine into the body and blood of Jesus, then that's what happens.
The bread and the wine look the same, but the Holy Spirit
makes them different than what they seem. And then the people
eat Him."

For Bertram, who ate flesh and blood bodies every day, this
concept felt affirming. Still, he didn't understand how the body
and blood of a human could at the same time be bread and wine.
And then there was the question of Jesus Himself. What was in
it for Him? Why would He want to become food for humans?
"He doesn't mind? It doesn't hurt Him?"

"Hurt Jesus? Lord, no!" Clancy embraced himself. "Jesus
doesn't mind! Why, he loves to feed us our daily bread! He *wants*
us to eat his body and drink his blood! He told his very best
friends that, during the last supper he had with them on the
night before he died. He took a cup of wine and blessed it, and
he said take this wine and drink it, because this is my blood. Do
this and remember me when I'm gone. And then he took a loaf
of bread and broke it, and he said this is my body, broken by the

sins of the world. Do this to remember me..." And before Clancy was half aware of what he was saying, he'd recited the Act of Consecration, having heard it so many times from the lips of Reverend DeBassompierre that he knew it quite by heart.

"Yum!" said Bertram, who had always wondered how human flesh might taste. "When do *we* get to do that?"

Clancy blinked. The question, posed with such uncomplicated trust by the buzzard, touched at the tender heart of the rodent's most intransigent uncertainties and insecurities, which were in the end one and the same. Certainly he believed that he was genuinely called by God, through Reverend DeBassompierre's example, to spread the Gospel and preach the Word. But to celebrate communion! That seemed like another level of ministry altogether, one for which he felt utterly unprepared. When in the past he'd observed, from his customary hiding place beneath the Hammond organ in the sanctuary, Reverend DeBassompierre's act of consecration, it was as if time stood still. There was always a moment when the handsome human priest, resplendent in his vestments, holding aloft the fractured wafer, seemed transfigured with a mysterious illumination, as if his own flesh, like the stained glass of the small round window above the altar, admitted a light from beyond. It was hard, terribly hard to believe, that he, Clancy, an orphaned rat, might possess that same quality of transparency to the Spirit. And yet, had not the Reverend DeBassompierre himself, in Clancy's original vision of his calling, ordered him to Feed His Sheep? Clancy opened his eyes to the curious, calm gaze of the young buzzard, and thanked the Lord for Bertram, who was clearly being used by the Spirit to encourage him.

"Bertram," he said. "You're right. We should have Holy Communion every Sunday."

"SILAS." Grace stood in the doorway of the Reverend DeBas-sompierre's office. She held in her hand a small cylindrical wax paper package. "We've got mice."

The Reverend DeBassompierre looked up from the huge concordance open on the desk before him. "What?"

"Mice!" said Grace. "Or rats. Whatever it is, it's been getting into the vestry cabinet, and you're not gonna believe this...but it's been taking off with the communion wafers." She placed the wax paper package in the spine of the open concordance. "Look at that. Chewed open on that end. And I'd say it made a good meal of about half the wafers. Unbelievable."

The Reverend picked up the compromised package and looked up at his secretary with astonishment. "Holy Mother of God! You're right!"

"Of course I'm right. Now. Do you want me to pick up some traps? Or do you want me to call a real professional? Because I'm telling you from experience, traps won't work for long. Those critters are smarter than they look. If you want my two cents, I think we need to bring in an exterminator."

Reverend DeBassompierre looked at the open package. He ran his finger along the chewed opening just beneath the glued seal and shook his head in wonder. "Can you beat that," he said. "I wonder what St. Francis would do?" He smiled a little.

"Call the exterminator, if he had any sense," said Grace. "So...?"

Reverend DeBassompierre's small smile lingered. "No," he said. "No, Grace, don't do that. We can't afford it, and anyway, I just don't like the idea of it. An exterminator in the sacristy...no, there's got to be some other way to handle it. We'll just start keeping the wafers in the fridge. That way they'll be safe." And he handed Grace the half-empty package and went back to his concordance.

Grace took the package, and then put her hands on her hips. "Silas. That's not going to solve the problem. It's not just about the communion wafers. I'm telling you, we have a rodent issue.

I've been suspecting as much for a long time. Listen to me. After I found this, I thought I'd check in the food pantry, and sure enough...a whole package of pop-tarts...nothing but wrappers and crumbs. Let me call the exterminator, Silas. You don't want these things getting bolder and coming out of the woodwork. How are you going to like it when one...or more...shows up in the middle of a service? If the vestry gets wind that the church is infested, they're gonna give you hell, and you know the first thing they'll do is blame it on the food pantry and the community garden, and shut the whole thing down. You're already on thin ice with the Warden as it is. Be smart, Silas. Let's nip this in the bud before it gets out of hand."

The young priest rubbed his forehead as if it ached. He swiveled a bit in his chair and looked toward the velvet cushioned prie-dieu in the corner of his office. Grace was right, of course. He couldn't afford to have vermin in the church. He sighed very deeply, and opened his mouth to tell Grace to do what she thought best. "Just try to get it done while I'm in Boston for the wedding so I don't have to see anything," he said. "Oh, and by the way, I'm going to need you to feed Macrina for me." He avoided looking at her, well aware that she was going to be upset by this last minute request, for he was leaving in the morning.

"Silas! You've got to be kidding me! I..." Grace was about to toss the half-empty packet of communion wafers right at her boss's head when he stood up, holding one finger aloft as if he'd received a prophetic word. "That's it!" he cried in triumph.

Grace's eye's widened. "What's it?"

"Macrina!" he said. "*She'll* keep out the mice! Why didn't I think of that!" He sat back down again, and Grace noted, with not a little alarm, that his normally somber eyes were bright, like those of a man with a mission.

"Silas, what are you talking about?"

"Macrina! Macrina, my cat! Instead of you having to drive all the way to my place this weekend, I'll just bring her here, and you won't have to make that extra drive! That way, we kill two birds...or two mice, ha ha...with one stone! You'll save time, and Macrina will guard the Sacrament! It's perfect!"

"Perfect except for the fact that you never asked me! Silas, can't you ask someone else? I've got a million things on my plate..."

The reverend looked down at his blotter. "Grace, I'm sorry. I know I should have thought about it before. But now I'm stuck. You know I don't have any friends in this town, Grace...please?"

Grace put her hands in her hair. "Silas, you have got to get your shit together. I'm your assistant, not your slave. Tommy's coming home this weekend, I have a paper due in my pastoral psychology class, and my car's acting up. You don't pay me enough for all this side work. I can't do it, Silas, I mean it. Can't you board her somewhere?"

Reverend DeBassompierre had, of course, thought of that. But something told him that Macrina would not take kindly to being warehoused with a bunch of other strange animals, even if she knew it was temporary. "I tried that; they're all full," he lied. "Please, Grace. I promise I'll never ask you to do anything extra again."

Grace Holbach gritted her teeth.

"I'm back in therapy, Grace. I really am trying. It's just been a...challenging couple of weeks. George's engagement has really thrown me..."

She scowled.

"Grace...please. I swear I'll make it up to you. I'll give you three vacation days...after the holidays...and I'll pay for your extra gas."

"That'll be the day," she said, but she was softening. Three days off for what amounted to two short extra trips wasn't a bad deal. "All right. But I'm not changing any litter."

"God bless you, Grace," said her boss.

Grace rolled her eyes and went back to her desk.

☙❧

THE FIRST COMMUNION Service celebrated at St. Aloysius Jr. was not, like the Baptismal Ceremony and the wedding, the seminal event that Clancy had expected. Nevertheless, he refused to be dismayed. The trouble was, that apart from Bertram and the opossums and himself, most members of the congregation found the communion wafers, which Clancy had helped himself to earlier in the week by sneaking into the sacristy cabinet, disagreeable to their particular digestive systems. Clancy, who, like Bertram, seemed to have a stomach of steel, could not imagine being unable to tolerate such bland fare, especially if it was God Himself! But even Ottoline, normally so cooperative, raised the issue, approaching him the next day to let him know that the Body of Christ had unfortunately caused her and Steven to experience painful bloating. She added that several squirrels, as well as the buck deer Magnus, had shared with her the same complaint.

Clancy wondered why those others had not spoken to him about this. At the same time he was not a little irritated that Ottoline was doing precisely that. Was it too much to expect that, as Christians, creatures would be willing to put up with a little indigestion for the sake of the Gospel? He already felt that he was cutting corners liturgically in that he was not offering the Blood of the New Covenant, but he hadn't figured out how to get any of it out of the bottle. It seemed to him that it was time to put his paw down. Gently, of course.

"I'm sorry to hear that," he said to Ottoline. "But I have to do as Jesus says. Maybe you'll get used to it."

"Maybe," Ottoline said, but she was very dubious. Still, there seemed to be no point in pressing the matter. If necessary, she would simply abstain, and that would be the end of it.

☙❧

AFTER GRACE SET out her tuna and her milk and left the building, Macrina sniffed and nibbled a bit, but she wasn't really hungry. To her mild surprise, although she knew it was only temporary, she found that it was not a little unsettling to be left all alone in such a big empty building. She'd become used to the cluttered spaces of the Reverend's townhouse and, what was more, to his quiet presence with her in the evenings. She missed him. She curled up on the horsehair cushion of the prie-dieu and tried to nap, but she was simply too keyed up. She spent a few minutes grooming herself, but when that was done she still felt restless. It occurred to her that she might feel more comfortable once she'd given the once over to the entire structure. She felt very sure that her clergyman would not have left it in a situation that would in any way pose a threat to her well-being...still, life had taught her the hard way that it was always better to be safe than sorry. She padded carefully out of the administrative wing, and made her way down the long corridor to the sanctuary, pausing at each closed door along each side to peer underneath. The sanctuary was large and dim and empty and yet seemed to her to be inhabited by a kind of pleasantly melancholy warmth, lent by the dying daylight as it was admitted and transformed into rich variegated colors by the stained glass windows. She wandered among the pews, and rubbed her face against each corner of the stone altar, where the scent and presence of her priest was very strong. This made her feel all the more at home within the church. She padded back down the narrow red carpet that ran between the division of the pews just before the altar, and was almost at the narthex, when she caught a sound, a scurrying sound, from the small room to the right of the altar, near the very back of the sanctuary.

Macrina didn't have to try to be stealthy; it was second nature. She padded swift and sure into the very dark little room. With its linoleum countertop and small sink, with cabinets above and beneath this counter, it reminded her very much of the Reverend's tiny kitchen back at the townhouse. It lacked only the humming refrigerator and seldom used stove. There was a folding table with one folding chair set against the wall opposite the counter, and Macrina landed on it with a silent leap. From there she could observe that one of the cabinets—the middle one above the small sink—was open, and from within she could hear that scurrying movement very clearly, as well as a soft, but audible squeaking voice. "Oh Lord! They're all gone! What am I going to do?"

Macrina knew very well that what she heard was the voice of not merely *a* rat, but *the* rat, the very rat that had, when she had simply wished to introduce herself and solicit some assistance, walloped her so brutally. What—or who—else could it be?! That same anxious energy, that same rather sour grainy scent filled the little room off the sanctuary. It didn't surprise Macrina one bit that the nasty creature had access to the interior of the church. After all, these rodents were by nature crafty little creatures who would stop at nothing to get what they wanted. She rested her haunches against the cool vinyl tabletop, and her pupils widened.

Clancy continued to lament to himself as he skittered in the dark cabinetry. "Oh Lord," he said. "I knew I should have taken the whole pack. I just didn't want to be greedy! Now they know. Oh Lord, what's gonna happen now?! I'm so *dumb!*" And as Macrina watched, the nasty creature emerged, snout, then head, then torso. It exited the open cabinet and dropped with a thump onto the countertop. It paused to look before leaping onto the floor from there, and then saw Macrina's amber eyes glinting in the dimness. And it shrieked, a high-pitched squeal that could storm heaven, but Macrina kept still.

"So you're the intruder," the cat purred. "I might have known."

Clancy gripped the edge of the countertop, terrified. He backed up instinctively against the wall, but he couldn't take his eyes off the cat.

"You aren't so tough now, are you, without all your friends around? Well, that's no surprise. Bullies never can stand on their

190 DAVID L. CARTER

own. I don't know what makes you think you have the right to just take what you want out of this place, but I'll have you know that I've been brought here to make sure nothing else goes missing. That's my duty, and I take it very seriously. Now, I am going to ask you one time, nicely, to remove yourself from this property, or I'll be forced to remove you myself. Do you understand?"

Up against the wall, Clancy regarded the beast crouched on the table.

"Get out," she said. "I'm not going to tell you again." She narrowed her eyes again, and this lent her countenance an air of stern authority that reminded Clancy of someone...but he was too scared to ask himself who.

"You're going to let me go?" he squeaked.

Macrina's whiskers stiffened with irritation. Was the creature hard of hearing? "I'm ordering you go!" she yowled. "You know full well that you are trespassing! You have no business in this place. And don't think I'm going to let you attack me again without any consequences. I may look pampered, but I can assure you, I know how to survive on the streets. I refuse to be bullied, and I refuse to fail to hold up my obligation to my keeper. I'm giving you one chance—now, take it! Or I won't be responsible for my actions."

Clancy could neither move nor speak. Even when he'd decided to approach the cat out in the churchyard and invite it to church, he'd never really imagined, he saw now, that it might really be civil. He shook himself from head to tail and crept forward slowly. "You aren't going to eat me? You're going to let me live?"

Macrina made a soft yacking noise. "Eat you! Don't be disgusting. I'm not some alley cat. I'm a pescatarian, for your information. I wouldn't eat a rodent if I was starving!"

Clancy blinked. He didn't know what a pescatarian was, but he did know that his Aunt November had made very sure he knew that he was to avoid cats at all costs, for they considered stout young rats the tastiest of morsels. And Aunt November wouldn't have lied. He backed up against the wall again. "Then why did you pounce me out in the playground?!" he challenged.

"Pounce you! You're the one who attacked me!"

Clancy felt as if he might be losing his mind. He reached for his tail and put it to his lips. Then, as if Hertz were watching him, he let it go. "That was that other rat," he said. "I was just going to invite you to join my church."

"What other rat?!" said the cat. "There was no rat but you. What a pathetic attempt to avoid taking responsibility. I suppose, then, it was this other rat who's been stealing communion wafers. Oh, I know all about what your 'other' rat has been up to in here. But I'm afraid that you're the only other rat I've seen, so you're the one that has to vacate. You should thank your lucky stars that the man in charge here elected to have me come in and patrol instead of calling an exterminator."

"Exterminator!" cried Clancy. "Oh Lord!"

Macrina was at once gratified by and felt a little guilty about the level of distress that this elicited in the rodent, who helplessly urinated right on the counter. After it had behaved so brutally out in the playground, what a ninny it was turning out to be, scared of its own shadow! In spite of herself she was beginning to feel a bit sorry for it.

"Look," she said. "I have no interest in making trouble for anybody. I know what trouble is. As long as nothing else goes missing, they'll figure I'm doing the trick, and then there won't be any more talk about exterminators. You go your way, and I'll go mine. All I want is peace and quiet, for myself and my very busy keeper. Believe me, I've had enough chaos for nine lives."

Clancy's squeak was breathless. "You really aren't going to eat me?"

"I told you, I would sooner starve!" Macrina was losing patience as quickly as she'd gained it. "And besides! I happen to have a very fancy feast waiting for me in the Reverend's office, which you are preventing me from enjoying!" She could hear the haughtiness in her own vocalization, and this made her soften.

She paused and, against her inclination, made a reluctant yet sincere overture. "I suppose there's enough for you as well, if you care to join me. At least you won't be stealing, for once."

Clancy was thoroughly bewildered. He had no faith that this cat, who had haunted his ministry from the very beginning, and for whom he'd overcome his own natural aversion in order to extend Christian witness—only to be spurned!—had any good will towards him. And for it, from its position of cossetted privilege, to characterize his only means of survival as stealing was really not nice. And yet, what choice did he have but to accept its invitation as his only hope?

The cat rose, descended from the table, and left the sacristy, and Clancy leaped down to the floor and followed, through the sanctuary, down the hall, across Grace's portion of the administrative suite, and into the Reverend DeBassompierre's office. There, by the prie-dieu, was set a dish of tuna and a bowl of milk.

"Help yourself," said Macrina primly. "There's a gracious plenty. I don't require much. I like to stay slim. The clergyman always complains that I never clean my plate."

The two creatures settled themselves across from one another at the setting and began to dine. Clancy found the tuna to be somewhat gamy for his taste, but he was not finicky. After the meal was finished, and the cat did not dismiss him, but simply proceeded to gaze at him with benign curiosity, Clancy felt emboldened to defend his actions. "You know, I only took those wafers so that my church could take communion just like they do. And how can we do that without communion wafers?"

"Well, I don't see why that's any excuse," said Macrina. "Just use something else."

Clancy leaped at what finally seemed to be an opportunity to demonstrate his theological acumen to this creature who, as agreeable as she was proving to be, still might benefit from being taken down a peg. "Oh, but you can't just use anything. See, the service says, 'On the night before He died, Jesus took the loaf of bread, and blessed it, and said Take, eat, this is my Body, Do this in remembrance of Me.' You'd know that if you ever saw him celebrate the Eucharist. I encourage you to attend one Sunday when he gets back in town."

"Oh, he blesses everything he eats," said Macrina offhandedly, "and everything I eat too. Apparently, you're not supposed to take it all so literally." Macrina yawned, rose, stretched languorously, and curled herself up upon the horsehair cushion of the prie-dieu. "Now, if you'll excuse me...I need my beauty rest. You're welcome to stay, but...I won't be much company."

Clancy's teeth ground, as he observed his nemesis and rival for Reverend DeBassompierre's affection and regard, lapse into an easy doze. It was easy for her to say he was taking things too literally...she wasn't a Reverend! Still...in his contrite heart he knew she might be right. He left the office of his dreams and made his way down to his damp, dim, fusty and moldy but familiar cellar, and planned the next Communion service.

CODA

"The Body of Christ, the Bread of Heaven." Clancy held aloft the sunflower seed that Ottoline had just a moment before placed reverently before him on the top surface of the altar/pulpit/composter, closed his eyes, then lowered it and placed it into his assistant's open beak. He then repeated the procedure with Steven.

"The Body of Christ, the Bread of Heaven." He held aloft the acorn, then lowered it and handed it back to Elwood, to divide and share with his mate.

"The Body of Christ, the Bread of Heaven." Holding his breath and swallowing his disgust, Clancy gingerly picked up the decomposing dead field mouse, lifted it up to the Lord, then placed it into the open beak of his dear friend Bertram, who swallowed it with an audible gulp.

"Amen!" said Bertram, adding, "Yum!"